For the three who were with me
for every step of the way
– S.F.

1

NOW

I can steal time.

The most I can take at the moment is fifteen seconds, which is not a lot. Grandmother took almost three minutes once and she told me she's done more, but I never saw it. And when she was tired, which was more and more often, or pretending not to be sad, which was pretty much always, she struggled to get to half that.

She says there are stories of someone who can take all the time in the world, but how can that be right? She said it when she was trying to get me to concentrate, when she was urging me to focus. As if all I had to do was understand what was possible to make it happen. It sounded unbelievable but when she said it there was a kind of memory in her eyes and something about her look that made me think maybe it was more than just a wild story.

And we didn't need all the time in the world, did we? We just needed enough to get to England. To fight and crash and tear our way to England where Dad said we would be safe. I hoped a few seconds might be enough to keep the two of us from getting caught but I guess I was wrong. We started with everything and I ended with nothing. On a beach in the dark; cold

wet and empty.

I should have practised more. Because every second is precious. And I never took enough.

2

AFTER

He grabs my collar and hauls me up the beach. There is anger in his grip and fear on his face, reflected yellow in the strange lamps that light the seafront path. He half runs and now he lets go, but I don't stop. Stones shift under my feet and my wet jeans rub hard against my legs but I don't slow down. We reach the tarmac and he swerves to the right, twisting briefly to check I am still there.

"Keep up," he says. But he doesn't need to.

I turn, briefly, as we hurry forward. Blue lights flash into the black sky and shouts rebound against the crash of the waves, behind the sounds of our hard breathing and the slap of our feet against the road. We run with the cliff to our left. Out in front is a deserted cafe, then a pool of light as the path turns up and away from the sea. There is a metal barrier to stop cyclists, then a pub car park, deserted except for a van and two large waste bins

And three police cars parked in a line like crooked teeth.

Ronnie lurches towards the cliff, gripping my arm and hauling me into some scrubby bushes hidden by the shadow. He curses, hard, under his breath then lies still, panting. I lie next to him, under the rough leaves, close enough to feel the heat of his body, staring up into the light. He takes a phone out his pocket and makes a call, whispering quickly to whoever answers.

"They're everywhere. Did you get out? How many were taken?"

He freezes as two policemen walk quickly past us back to the beach. Then he lies still.

"How many?" I whisper.

"You speak English?" He sounds surprised.

"Yeah. How many?"

"All of them," he says.

I feel the wave of fear rushing through me. Ice burns in my stomach. Panic fills my mind.

"What do we do?"

"We get out of here."

"What about my dad?" I whisper.

"We get out of here," he says again. "Then we find out."

We watch the policemen disappear into the blur of the lights under the cliff then turn back to the way ahead.

"OK. When I say run, we run," Ronnie says. "As fast as you can. Past the cars then up that road. There is a church. Turn left and look for a black BMW. A friend of mine is waiting and will drive us away."

"Is that your plan?" I ask.

He nods then braces himself to move. I put my hand on his arm to stop him.

"That's a terrible plan," I hiss. "You want to get caught?"

He stares at me, surprise and a hint of anger in his eyes. I feel his body tense again as he readies himself to run, but I lean across and push him down flat.

"What do you know about getting caught?" he hisses. "You are just a foreign kid to them. It's all good if they catch you. I am a man. I have a life here. It's different for me."

"So what?" I whisper. "I'll come up with a plan that isn't terrible. Just let me think."

I calm my breathing and still my thoughts like she showed me. I concentrate on doing nothing, filling my mind with my own image, lying still in the undergrowth. I am doing nothing while the world turns around me. I am locked in place.

I creep forward until I can hear voices and the buzz of radios. Somewhere, a phone goes off, but I ignore it and crawl to the edge of the light. And then I burst out, running as fast as I can, like the winds of hell are on my back. I make it to the cars before the police react, then I swerve to the left. A woman officer stares at me, then yells, and all the heads turn at once. I duck to the left, swerving round with my hand on a car bonnet, pushing shut the car door before the man can get out. I accelerate into the street Ronnie showed me, ignoring the shouts, ignoring the threats, ignoring the burning in my muscles as I tear up the road.

Until a man crashes into my legs and we tumble over. I try to scramble free but he has me tight. Another officer arrives and yanks my hands hard behind my back. I feel metal round my wrists then they haul me to my feet.

I roll on to my back and stare into the darkness. "We can't do it your way," I hiss. "It won't work."

Ronnie is nervous. He wants to run, but it is the wrong thing to do. "Trust me," I say. "The police will have you in less than fifteen seconds. Wait here," I insist. "They may go in a minute."

They won't go in a minute, but it is what I need to say to stop him running. I look again at the cars. There were two officers in the car on the left, another behind it and the last two standing between the cars. So there is more space to the right. I calm myself again and concentrate, waiting until my heart is still. I am locked in place.

I creep forward until I can hear voices and the buzz of radios. Somewhere, a phone goes off, but I ignore it and crawl to the edge of the light. And then I burst out, running as fast as I can, like the winds of hell are on my back. I make it to the cars before the police react, then swerve to the right. A woman officer turns, moving instinctively but then hesitating, because her view is blocked by the other cars. Then she yells and all the heads turn at once. I race round the right-hand car, leaning on the bonnet, then accelerating away. I hear the slam of a door from the other side, then shouts behind me and footsteps as they give chase. Then the burst of an engine.

I turn into the street Ronnie showed me, forcing my body faster as I see the church up ahead. I turn left as a car pulls alongside me, blue light spilling over the street as its tyres screech. I see the BMW parked ahead.

The police car slews across the road in front of me. I swerve but can't avoid it, rolling up over the bonnet then hitting the ground hard. The door opens and I see a dark uniform as it crashes down on top of me, rolling me over and yanking my hands hard behind my back. I feel metal round my wrists then they haul me to my feet.

I roll over again and stare out in front. Ronnie hisses at me. "You move too much," he says. "Keep still."

I glare at him and think about going on my own but I need this guy for now. "OK," I say. "Here's what we do. We creep forward on the right-hand side until I say, then we run, as fast as we can. I will be behind you but don't slow down."

He looks at me like I'm insulting him. "That is just as terrible as my plan," he says. "We do it—"

But I grab his shoulder to interrupt him. "WAIT!" I hiss. "Turn your phone off!"

Panic fills his eyes and he yanks his phone up and flicks it to silent just as it starts buzzing.

"How did you—?" he starts, but I ignore him.

"We do my plan," I say. "Let's go."

I am gone before he can argue, creeping forward until I can hear voices and the buzz of radios, crawling right up to the edge of the light. I push Ronnie in front of me, then count down – three, two, one – and we burst out, running as fast as we can, like the winds of hell are on our back. We make it to the cars before the police move, then swerve to the right. A woman officer turns, moving instinctively but then hesitating, because her view is blocked by the other cars. Then she yells and all the heads turn at once. We race round the right-hand car, Ronnie leans on the bonnet, then accelerates away. I charge at the blue bin by the pub wall and pull on its handle with all my might. It comes away and crashes down behind the car, but I don't slow down. I hear the slam of a door from the other side, then shouts behind me and footsteps as they give chase. Then the burst of an engine, followed by a crunch as the police car reverses into the bin.

I turn into the road behind Ronnie, forcing my body faster as I see him turn at the church up ahead. I see the BMW doors open and I dive into the back. The wheels spin and the car pulls away, slowing only as we pass the police car looking for two pedestrians. I tip my head back against the headrest and gasp the cold English air in relief.

The journey is over.

3

BEFORE

It's a victory I need to win. For the underdog against the forces of oppression. I stare at her with a face as innocent as water.

She stares at me with an expression of tranquillity and love.

We take deep breaths and wonder how to destroy the other within the rules of classroom engagement. Eyes lock, plans are made and battle lines drawn. I will never surrender.

OK, maybe "forces of oppression" is a bit harsh because I know she cares about us really. And she does help me a lot with my languages, which are the only subjects I'm any good at, but on a bad day she can be pretty oppressive. Like if you forget your homework or if you're just having a bit of a chat at the back of the class when she's talking. And we all need victories, don't we?

She moves first.

"No, that isn't what I was going to say, Aleksander," she lies. "Now, who can tell me the English word for 'fa—'"

"Factory," I say.

Her eyes narrow. She can't decide if she actually said it or not. Davos, who sits next to me, can't either.

He raises his eyebrows at me but I don't move. If I could look more helpful I'd be a library.

She gives that one to me. "Yes, that's right," she says. One-all. "What about the English for 'z—'"

"Spare parts," I say.

Somebody behind me giggles in the way that only thirteen-year-olds can. I hear the word "cheating" whispered, but I can't be, can I? I just have that strange knowledge of what's coming the moment before it arrives, like I always have. Two-one to me.

She smiles. Time to be careful.

"Last one," she says. "Who knows the English word for…" She hesitates, deliberately. We smile at each other. She opens her mouth again. "'Zat—'"

"Detention," I say quickly. The girls at the back all laugh together. Davos is staring at me, wondering what's going on. Three-one and game, I'm thinking.

"Very good, Aleksander," she says. "Detention it is. See me at the end of the lesson."

How can I win if she can change the rules?

"I don't know how you do it, Alex," she says, but she is smiling as she picks up her notes and puts them into her case.

"My dad worked for three years in England, miss,"
I say.

"Yes, I know why your English is good, but I still don't
know how you do it. You have a gift for languages
almost like you know what people will say before they
say it!" She perches on the edge of her desk and takes
off her glasses. "I'm going to miss these lessons."

For a moment I don't understand what she is saying
until I feel that lurch in my stomach.

"Are you leaving?"

"You didn't already know?" she says in mock
surprise. She rubs her glasses on a cloth and sighs.
"We're leaving the country," she says. "Going back to
America. I don't feel safe like I used to."

"I'm sorry, miss," I say, and I guess I really am. For a
moment I wonder if I have done something to drive
her away, but I don't know what it could be. I guess
leaving is just what people do.

"Do I really need to do detention?" I ask. "It's just
that I've got football practice."

She looks out of the window for a moment, at the
grey clouds filling up the sky, then shakes her head.

"I will miss you, Aleksander," she says. "Take care of
yourself, won't you? And promise me you'll give your

next teacher a chance."

I promise, and I just know she is going to try and hug me, so I step out of the way slightly. Then I am halfway out of the door before she wipes the shine away from her eyes. I've got games to play and goals to score and a bike that needs racing and trees to climb and a river and hills and woods and a whole world to tear apart then put back together so I will be fine.

But she is gone within a week.

The new kids start arriving a week after that. A new headmistress to replace old Levan, although maybe he wasn't that old. English lessons stop and we start Mandarin. The girl, Mariam, who held my hand once on a trip to the caves, leaves without saying goodbye. I work hard because I have a strange feeling that I need to. Summer turns into autumn.

A boy I don't recognise at school calls me a name. The others laugh. Then it's a shove in the playground, hard into my shoulder, as I'm playing football. Too deliberate for me to get out of the way, knocking me off balance so I go flying. I scream foul, but they play on. I can still see the tackles coming but they are harder to avoid. I score the most goals by far, but I lose my place in the team.

Time goes by and now I have a nickname. I tell Dad and he looks up sharply. I don't mention it again.

One Wednesday morning, another kid is pulled out of the crowd. He is younger than me, but I know him because he came to the house with his dad once. He stands in the middle of a circle of noise, mud on his shirt, fear in his brown eyes. For a moment I think about walking away, but I don't. I yell at them to stop and now I am next to him. A girl shouts something about us all being the same, but I've hardly ever met this boy next to me. Someone else throws something. A sandwich hits his face. I sense something coming and I move, then spin round to see my friend Davos looking on, red-faced. I raise my fists, then the teacher comes.

Davos sits next to me the next day and I tell him to go to hell. The day after that I am moved to the back. I have more room to spread my books out.

Dad has to come and see the headmistress. He waits while her assistant brings her some tea, then nods when she says she doesn't have long. I have been fighting. It is not acceptable behaviour. I have been unruly and disturbing the other kids. If he wants me to do well in the new system he must control me. Where is my mother? Well, perhaps that was to be expected. As is bad behaviour, but she will not tolerate it at her school.

I watch Dad's fingers resting on his knees. They pinch the fabric of his trousers tight, so that the white shows in his knuckles. He hardly speaks. He doesn't ask any questions.

He doesn't ask me any questions on the way home either. I start to tell him that it wasn't my fault but he just says I need to get used to things being difficult. We get in and he speaks to Grandmother briefly. In low tones that I can't hear. Then he goes out and Grandmother comes in. She brushes my hair away from my eyes with her fingers and tells me not to worry. She says Dad is doing his best but things are tough at the moment. I know things are happening but nobody really explains what they are. And I don't want to make it worse so I stay as quiet as I can.

A boy in the class below is not at school. There

are gaps in the form lines. Someone has scrawled something on the school wall and we are made to line up until someone admits to it. Feeling passionate about something does not justify any behaviour, the headmistress says. The guilty must come forward, but nobody does. Very well. She will assume it was the children with the most disruptive records, and if it isn't fair, we should learn to have respect for authority. Five of us are given a bucket and a brush and an afternoon.

But we would never use those words.

I am hurt this time. Too bad to hide. I see the blows coming, but there are too many to dodge and when they win a fight at last, they make It count. The cold seeps into my body as I lie on the ground and stare at the railway tracks where they threw my phone. I can't tell Dad I've lost it. And it just keeps ringing.

I can't run easily because my leg is dead but the trains go so fast. The red stones crunch under my shoes. The icy ground is hard as I stumble.

I run down the bank straining my ears for the sound of...

But it is only a glimpse. I run down the bank and

almost cry out as I jump and land hard, grabbing the phone, then forcing myself away. The train doesn't come.

"Yes, I'm fine," I tell my dad. "I'll be back soon. I had to do something before coming home."

At night I listen as Dad and Grandmother argue. "His gift is starting to come through," she says, but this seems to make things worse.

Dad growls. "There are bigger things than him at the moment," he says. "There are more important things than stupid tricks. Don't you realise the risks I am taking? We just need to keep our heads down and stay out of trouble."

I will stay out of trouble, I say to the frost on the windowpane.

I will do everything you ask me to.

Dad comes home early. "They are reorganising things and there will be fewer shifts," he says. "Of course, it's only temporary – there's always work at the post office. Yes, I know that's what I said before but it is different now. Of course it's nothing to do with the school," he snaps.

He tells me he's sorry and reaches out to put his hand on my shoulder for a moment. Then he goes out.

I sit with my back against the bedroom door. If I am still I can hear the low voices. "Maybe it's time to go," he says, and I feel the ice freeze inside me. Then I breathe again.

"This is our home," she says. "And things must get better. It's a different world now. Internet, pictures, stories. People must know, and they will put it right, won't they?"

But he doesn't answer.

Our retired neighbours are arrested. Their son gets drunk and tears up the police station. Guns are drawn, then fired. A funeral is not permitted and they don't come back. The house remains empty.

Dad calls me in and tells me to sit down. "Do you know what's happening in our country, Alex?" he asks.

"I don't know," I say. "I hear what people say."

He nods. "Our home isn't what it was," he says. "There is a war that the world doesn't know about and we don't know how to win."

"What should we do?"

"We fight, in the best way we can," he says. "Does that frighten you?"

I nod. "But you once said you can't be brave unless you are scared."

He smiles for a moment. "You were always brave," he says. "That was something." He leans forward in his chair so it feels like we are close together. "I may have to leave soon," he says. "If I do, I want you to look after your grandmother."

I hesitate as the words seem to enter my body like a knife. He frowns and waits for an answer. "I can fight," I say.

"You are a child," he says, "and this isn't a war for the brave, it's a war for the clever. Because we are up against an enemy who won't let us tell anyone what is happening." He shakes his head. "If I go, I need you to stay here with your grandmother."

"Will you come back?"

"Of course," he says, and the conversation is over.

But I know this isn't true. Because I've heard it before.

4

AFTER

I wake up from dreams of panic; seabirds screaming and the black water sucking me in. Ronnie kicks at my feet from where they are sticking over the end of the sofa and I lurch forward with wide eyes.

"Time to get up," he says.

My back hurts. I pull the thin blanket round my shoulders. "Is there any news?" I ask. "What time is it?"

He pulls back the grimy curtains and grey light spills into the room. "Ten o'clock, and there is no news," he says. "But you must speak English now, even to me. Is your English good enough?"

"My English is perfect," I say in English.

He grunts and steps into the light. Blond hair cut short, stained white teeth, the tattoo of a dragon winding out of his white shirt collar up his neck, ready to breathe fire.

He perches on a hard wooden chair and stares across at me. "It's time to go," he says.

"I need to find my dad..." I start, and when I say the words I feel so sick I can hardly finish the sentence. "Otherwise it's all been for nothing."

He shakes his head. "If your dad's alive he'll be with the authorities. But it will take a week before you hear anything."

"If he's alive?"

Ronnie doesn't say anything and I bite down the panic rising inside me. I don't know how injured he was and I can't think about it.

"He must be alive," I say. "We made a plan for if we got separated."

Ronnie shakes his head. "No one else got off the beach. So if they took him they will send him back," he says. "There is no reason for them to let people from our country stay."

"We can't go back. People are going missing. We need to show the British what's happening."

Ronnie sighs and he leans back in the chair. "Has it got that bad?"

"I thought you knew. I thought that's why you helped me. I saw you talking to my dad."

He shakes his head and looks down. "He gave me money to keep you safe," he says.

"We didn't have any money. It was all gone."

"There is always more money. Something valuable hidden away. It is my job to get it. That is why they pay me."

"I was watching," I say. "He didn't give you any money."

Ronnie holds my gaze for a moment then looks away. He lifts his left hand to his mouth and bites at his nails, then he hesitates, glancing down and switching fingers to one that looks just as bitten as the others. Then he gets up and walks into a small kitchen and I sit up and pull on my jeans.

"There are things I need to do. That will help my dad."

He shrugs. "Fine," he says. "But you must go soon. I have work to do."

"There are documents I need to get that will help him. From a post office in London." When he doesn't answer, I find my eyes drifting around the tidy flat, at the battered box of toys in the corner and the crayon drawings pinned on the wall. If we want to stay, I need to get Dad's documents. Otherwise everything has been wasted.

"I need help," I say.

He snorts. "I can't help you," he says. "There are thousands who want to come here. They all want help. They all offer me nothing in return."

He seems determined. His arms are crossed and his jaw is set, but I don't know how to last a week on my own and he is the only person I know. "Maybe there is something I could offer you," I say, trying not to sound desperate. "I have talents. I could help with your work."

"What I do is not for kids," he says scornfully. "It is hard and people get hurt."

"That is why you need my help."

He leans back and laughs, stretching his arms out across the back of the chair. "Your dad said you were a little bear," he says. "Have you got teeth, Little Bear? Can you fight off the other bears?"

"I protected you on the beach last night," I say. "If I hadn't, you would have been caught."

And this stops him laughing. He leans forward and his eyes narrow. "What do you mean?" he says.

I am not sure what to say. Grandmother said to never tell a stranger. Dad said to keep it a secret, but I have nothing else. I rack my brains.

"We make a good team," I say, "and I am good at reading people. Why don't you let me help you?"

He scoffs. "What are you talking about?"

"I have a gift for listening," I say. "I can tell if people are lying. I bet I can tell if you tell me a lie."

He laughs – a short, gunshot of a laugh – but there

is curiosity in his eyes. "OK," he says. "But if you are messing me around ..." He doesn't finish.

"Tell me something," I say. "And I will tell you if you are telling the truth."

He thinks for a moment. "I have four brothers," he says.

I force myself to look at him, then I try to look through him, staring into the distance, making my mind blank. I let my thoughts calm, almost feeling the emptiness fill me. I concentrate my mind on myself, like I am watching myself sitting in front of him. I sit completely still. I am locked in place.

"True," I guess.

He shakes his head, the anger spilling out of his eyes. "This is stupid," he says. "You need to leave."

"That's not true," I say.

He nods slowly. "I have three brothers," he says with a thin smile, "and they all want to come to England. A lucky guess maybe," he continues. "Next question. I have five pound coins in my pocket."

"True," I guess again.

He nods.

"True," I say.

"My father's name was Michael."

"False."

"I don't like carrots."

"Not true," I say. "How else do you see so well in the dark?"

He grunts. "My favourite film is *Inception*."

"True," I say. "But I'm sure you'd like *Moana* if you only gave it a chance."

He looks up sharply and for a moment I wonder if I have gone too far. But then he smiles and keeps going. Statement after statement, like a game where he's desperate for me to fail, but I never get one wrong. Eventually he runs out of things to say and halts. I start to speak but he holds up a hand to stop me.

"I once shot a man," he says.

The question shocks me but I try not to show it. I concentrate again, sitting completely still, not knowing if I want to know the answer. I am locked in place.

"True."

He nods slowly, then sighs and leans back in the chair.

"Here or at home?" I ask.

"Why does that matter?" he asks, but then he relents. "It wasn't here," he says. "And now I can never

go back. A soldier was going to kill an innocent man and I wanted to stop him. There was a fight and there was a gun and I just grabbed it and it went off." He shrugs.

"True," I say. "But you didn't mean to do it. It was an accident."

"How do you..." he starts, but then he waves the question away, leaning back in his chair and staring at me thoughtfully. I sit in silence, holding his gaze. He bites at one of his nails, his eyes narrowing as he tries to work out what to do with me. Eventually he seems to make a decision.

"OK, Little Bear," he says. "You have some kind of trick, but it works. Maybe I can use that." He nods slowly. "I am meeting someone. I need to know if they are telling me the truth or if they are the police."

"I should be able to do that."

But now he scowls. "'Should' isn't good enough," he says. "I need to know if these people are straight. 'Should' could get me killed, and then where would you be?"

"Is it to do with something illegal?" I ask, but he just laughs.

"Of course it's something illegal," he says. "Who

30

gives people like us proper jobs? Now can you do it, or do you want to get out and wait for the police to pick you up?"

I don't know what else to do. "I can do it," I say. "But you need to help me if I do."

He bites his nails again as he looks at me. Then he nods. "OK," he says. "If you help me, I will pay you one hundred pounds. Enough to go to your post office and wait for your dad. But if you screw this up..."

The words hang in the air, but I have nothing in my pockets and nowhere to go.

What else can I do?

5

BEFORE

I am sitting in the kitchen. Dad is out and Grandmother and I will both be tense until he is back. She tells me to concentrate, but I can't and I tell her I want to stop. Then she snaps at me louder and more angrily than I expect; harder than seems right.

"Aleksander!" she barks. "What is the point of having a gift if you won't learn to use it?"

I feel like she's slapped me.

And she isn't concentrating either. We have been working for ages now, and her eyes keep flicking to the television. The noise roars again and people are shooting. She turns the TV off.

"Maybe you are too young," she says. "But there is no one else to teach you and I may not have long left."

"Are you leaving too?" I ask, and she must see the fear in my eyes because she shakes her head quickly.

"No," she says, but then she hesitates. She gets up from the table where we have been sitting and walks to the window, staring at the weeds that stain the small garden like the brown marks on her hands. Then she sighs.

"Tell me," I say, but when she turns back I wish I had not asked.

Her hand moves to her side but I don't think she

realises I've noticed. I see the shadow under the bright eyes and the prominence of the bones in her face.

"Are you unwell?" I ask, but she scowls.

"Do not use it on me!" she snaps.

"I thought you wanted me to practise."

She holds my gaze for a moment, then laughs a little but there is a sadness in it. She comes back from the window. "Give me a hug," she says, waiting until I go to her. She is small in my embrace and I feel uncomfortable but she holds me for what seems like an age. Her hair is almost white, but her arms are still strong.

"We are not all like your mother," she says quietly. "And we are not all scared of things we don't understand."

I don't reply and eventually she sighs. "Yes, I am not so well," she says. "So we must make the most of our time."

"Will you go to hospital?" I ask, but she shakes her head.

"They are busy with the soldiers," she says. "And I don't want to be there." She sighs and gestures to the TV. "Everything is turning to dust," she says. "And you must be careful."

I shrug. "I have never told anyone," I say. "I don't even talk to Dad."

She nods and looks away. "He has a lot on his mind right now," she says. "And he is scared. You must keep practising."

She shuffles round the table and sits down. "Let's start again," she says, lining the dominoes up. "This isn't magic and it's not going to just come to you. You can glimpse what might happen in the future but it is no strange power that allows this." She leans forward and stares at me. "Think again about the dominoes. What happens when we knock the first one down?"

I sigh because we have been over this a million times. "They all fall down," I say.

"That's right," she says quickly. "And you know what is going to happen even before it reaches the last one, don't you, because you know what is going to happen to each of them along the way, right?"

I nod.

"It is not magic or destiny that makes the last one fall. It is the rules of the world. You need to concentrate on seeing the path that leads from the first to the last before the tiles fall. Then you can do the same with everything else. Everything that happens is a reaction to what has happened before. And because everything in the world has to obey the laws of science, everything can be predicted."

She knocks over the first tile and we watch as they rattle over. "Just like these," she says, and then she smiles and lowers her voice until it is almost a whisper. "There is no such thing as magic," she says. "The future of the universe is written. And a few people in our family have a gift so they can learn to read it.

"Don't waste yours," she adds. "Because one day it might be the only thing you have."

6

AFTER

Ronnie tells me to hurry as I shove my feet into my trainers and pull on my jacket. I don't know what he expects, and fear gnaws at me that I won't be able to do it. Grandmother had three minutes. I only have fifteen seconds. Whatever Ronnie wants me to do is going to need more than a trick.

I just hope fifteen seconds will be enough.

Ronnie goes ahead of me down the stairs, talking on his phone, giving orders, shouting at someone to get things ready. Outside, two men are waiting in the black BMW. Music thumps out into the street.

The one in the passenger seat is the driver with a gold tooth from last night and he looks at me like he can't work out what's going on. The other one's just banging his head to the bass; dark, round sunglasses covering his eyes as if they were empty black holes in his skull. I get in the car without saying anything and Gold Tooth spins round sharply.

"What's going on?" he says. "Why've you brought the kid?"

But Ronnie doesn't answer him. He tells me to move along the back seat and scrambles in after me. "Get back to the yard," he says, and the car pulls out.

I stay silent as we drive parallel to the sea, the front windows down, the back windows up, until we reach a busy town and turn right, away from the seafront, and cruise up narrow streets buzzing with pedestrians. Ronnie chews his nails. Shades is swearing at the people walking in front of him. Gold Tooth has his arm out of the window and seems to be looking for someone in the crowds. Then suddenly we stop.

A man in a striped red T-shirt walks up to the car so casually that I don't even notice, until he drops a black rucksack through the open window, then walks away fast. Gold Tooth passes it back quickly to Ronnie, who opens it, revealing several plastic bags inside, and a gun. I stare at the metal, feeling like my blood has stopped pumping in my veins, until Ronnie sees me looking and shuts the bag quickly. He tells Shades to keep driving then looks at me and shrugs. Then he returns to biting his nails.

We drive until the streets are quieter, until we eventually get to a scrap-metal yard where a battered sign advertises refurbished gaming machines. When the car stops, Ronnie gets out, dragging me with him. Gold Tooth and Shades follow us. Ronnie strides forward into a small temporary office that looks like it's been there for about a hundred years, then drops the bag on the small desk and tells Gold Tooth and Shades to wait outside.

Shades stares at me before he goes. "What's with the kid?" he asks.

Ronnie bites his nails. "He's family. He's joining the crew. He'll be OK."

Shades doesn't look happy but he seems to accept it and just shakes his head as he leaves the office. Ronnie takes the gun out of the bag, doing something to it so that it clicks. Then he looks at me.

"You cool, Little Bear?" he says quietly.

"What do you want me to do?" I ask.

"You need to tell me if anyone lies to me," he says. The hand not holding the gun rises to his mouth quickly and bites one of his nails. His skin is shining with a faint trace of sweat and I realise he is still scared of something.

"I've got business with some people," he says. "But I don't know them and there've been raids recently. So you're going to tell me if these people are straight, aren't you?"

I don't answer until I realise he is waiting for me

to. I nod.

"Say, 'Yes, Ronnie,'" he says.

"Yes, Ronnie," I say.

"You're going to do that Baba Yaga mind-reading of yours and warn me before any money changes hands," he says. "And you need to do it without the others knowing what you're doing, right?"

I nod.

"Say, 'Yes, Ronnie,'" he repeats, and I say it.

He pulls back the top part of the gun and it makes a kind of snapping noise. "Because if they think I'm relying on kids and mind-reading they'll kill me, then they'll kill you, understand?"

He points the gun at me. "Say, 'Yes, Ronnie,'" he says again, and I say it.

He looks at me for a moment and I just stare at the small circle of blackness at the end of the barrel.

"When they come in here, you sit in the corner and keep your mouth shut. The only thing I want to hear from you is if we've got a problem."

He leans back and bangs on the thin metal office wall, then opens a drawer in the desk and slides the gun into it, along with the plastic packets. The door to the office opens and Shades is there. Ronnie leans in closer to me.

"And don't forget," he whispers. "If we do get raided, they'll take you too. And the journey back will be a lot quicker than the journey here."

The others come back in, but I don't look at them. Everyone is on edge; Ronnie is going from finger to finger, gnawing at the bitten stumps like a rat. Gold Tooth leans back in a chair, apparently looking at his phone, but with his eyes darting towards the door every few seconds, even though there is no sound from outside. Shades is sitting at the back of the office listening to music, arms crossed, leaning forward and rocking slightly in time with the tinny buzzing from his earbuds. And I just sit here wondering why I ever said I could tell if people are lying.

Because I can't, can I? I can only take fifteen seconds, and now I don't know how it can help me. Now I wish I'd practised for every moment there was, but I didn't. Someone thumps on the office door and everybody tenses. It's showtime and all I've got is fifteen seconds.

It isn't going to be enough.

Ronnie nods at Gold Tooth, who opens the door, letting in a man and a woman. Ronnie's eyes flick up to catch mine. Shades sees him staring at me and his eyes narrow. Then Ronnie stands up and tells Gold Tooth to wait outside. He leans forward with his hands on the desk and looks at the man who's entered.

"Who's this, Max?"

"Rachel," the woman answers, in a voice that sounds like she has scraped the edges off her words. She's white with brown hair tied back fiercely so it is tight against her face. She looks like she's in her thirties, with hard eyes and pale skin, wearing baggy blue jeans and a T-shirt. Ronnie has turned to look at her. Now he turns back to Max, but she moves so she's in the way.

"I'm the one you'll be dealing with," she says. "You got the goods?"

Ronnie hesitates, then he smiles, but he still looks wary. "Are you a good girl, Rachel?" he asks.

She holds his gaze. "Course I am," she says. "And I've got the money. You got the goods?"

She pulls a fat brown envelope out of a shoulder bag and shows it to him, but she doesn't let him take it. She waits while he opens the drawer and takes out the plastic packets and drops them on to the table. Jewellery spills out. Rachel pokes it about, sorting it quickly into two piles, one of gold and one of other items. "Some of this is junk," she says. "But I can do something with the gold." She picks up something from the first pile and lifts it up to the light, and as she does, I feel a sudden lurch in my stomach. I realise I've half stood up. Shades is staring at me, and now Ronnie turns to look at me too. His eyes widen and a sudden look of panic crosses his face.

"What is it?" he asks, and now everyone in the small room is staring at me. "What is it?" he repeats. "Something I need to know?"

But there isn't. I shake my head quickly, watching his eyes narrow in frustration. He looks down at my grandmother's necklace, which sparkles in Rachel's fingers before she tosses it in the no-good pile.

Shades laughs. "Maybe the kid thinks it will go with his eyes," he says.

But he doesn't know, does he? And maybe he wouldn't care if he did. But I remember her expression and I realise I have nothing else to remember her by. So I'm going to find a way to get it back. Even if I don't know how.

"What's with the kid anyway?" Rachel asks. "Some sort of bring-your-son-to-work day?"

Ronnie stares at her, trying to work out if she's insulting him. Eventually he grunts. "Let's just get on with it," he says, then he turns to me, his voice full of menace. "You shut up and do what you're told, kid, remember?"

His eyes linger on me a little longer than they need to and I know he is telling me to hurry up, but I still don't know what to do. I know fifteen seconds is not going to be enough but I have to try. I glance at the clock on the wall just as the second hand reaches the number ten. I focus my mind and lock myself in place.

Rachel prods at the smaller bags on the desk, tipping one of them up, and I watch as gold jewellery spills out on to the plastic surface in front of her. I stand up and push forward, ignoring the surprised look on Shades's face and how Max suddenly stands up straight. Rachel is prodding a number of rings and necklaces with her finger and now she is staring at me with her mouth wide open. I grab her shoulder and spin her round.

"You're a cop," I yell. "You're a cop, aren't you?"

Behind her the second hand ticks round to the eleven. I push her back into Max, still screaming at her that she's a cop. Max's hand reaches towards his waistband. Rachel is staring at me in shock. Ronnie is on his feet. Shades is reaching forward to grab my shoulder.

The second hand gets to the twelve.

I am pulled back, hard. Rachel rips my hand away from her shoulder and stares at me, but there is nothing in her eyes. Ronnie's hand is sliding open the desk drawer. Max is holding a gun. He points it at my head.

"What the hell's going on?" Rachel demands.

The second hand ticks round to the one.

"So are we doing this or what?" Rachel says. "How much is here?"

"Four kilos, give or take," Ronnie says.

"Give or take what?"

Ronnie smiles. "You give me the money or I take it all away," he says.

Rachel smiles back, then her expression hardens. "So let's do it," she says.

Ronnie glances at me, then back at her. He shrugs. "OK," he says.

"I'll give you three for the passports and thirty for the jewellery," Rachel says.

I look at the hands of the clock. And focus my mind again..

"She's a cop," I say.

Max straightens instantly. His hand flies to his waistband. Rachel takes a step back, her face full of shock. Ronnie stares at her for a moment, then leaps to his feet.

"How do you know?" he asks.

"I just know," I say.

Six seconds have passed.

"What's going on, Max?" demands Ronnie. "You bring a cop to my place?"

"She's not, I swear," says Max.

"Of course I'm not," Rachel spits.

Ten seconds. Now eleven.

Ronnie turns to me. "Are you sure?"

Thirteen seconds. I am locked in my mind, but I am losing it and I can feel time spreading out like a cloud of steam in the air.

"Are you sure?" Ronnie demands.

I ignore him, concentrating on watching Rachel's face and holding the world still. Fifteen seconds is gone, now sixteen, but she gives nothing away. And then there is something in her eyes...

But I don't know what it is.

"This stuff's worth twice that," Ronnie says. "Why are you wasting my time?"

Rachel shrugs. "Most of this is rubbish," she says. "Bits and pieces; low quality."

Ronnie glances across at me again and all I can think about is how I need to act before the money changes hands.

"Forty for the jewellery and five for the passports," says Rachel. "Or I walk away now."

Ronnie hesitates and looks at me with such anger in his eyes I know I have to do something. He reaches down and slides open the drawer.

I stand up.

"I need a word," I say, looking at Ronnie.

Shades is half on his feet. Rachel is staring at me like I'm insane. Ronnie looks worried, but I have his attention.

"Now?" he asks seriously.

"Yes," I say.

"What's going on?" Rachel asks, but I ignore her.

My heart is pounding in my chest. I'm in real time and there are guns in the room, but there's no going back now. Everyone is staring at me but I ignore

them and walk round the desk to Ronnie's side. I stare
down at where the drawer is open in front of me.

*I pick up the gun, flicking off the safety catch like
Ronnie did earlier.*

"She's a police officer," I shout.

*Max reaches for his waistband but I scream at him
that I will shoot if he touches his gun.*

"Put the gun on the desk," I yell, keeping Ronnie's
gun trained on Rachel. "Do it now!"

*Shades is on his feet, but Ronnie waves at him to
sit. Max holds the gun by the barrel and puts it on the
desk then moves back against the wall. Ten seconds
have gone past.*

I stare at Rachel. "You're police, aren't you?" I yell.
"Admit it. You're police, aren't you?"

*She doesn't answer. The room is quiet. Fifteen,
sixteen, seventeen, eighteen. I am at my limit.*

I have no more time.

7

BEFORE

"Aleksander, you need to trust me," she snaps. "And you need to trust yourself. Otherwise you will never have more than moments."

I push my chair back, scraping it along the stone floor so it screeches like a pig in the way she hates, and I watch as her jaw tenses. "What's the point?" I say. "I can't do it. It's just a waste of time."

She stands too, but she is still looking up at me. "Do you have any idea—" she starts, but she doesn't finish. The front door slams.

I look up at the clock on the kitchen wall but it is still early. I move towards the hall door but she puts her arm out to stop me.

"Wait here," she says. "I'll go."

Footsteps come thumping up the stairs. Then Grandmother's voice, calling out. Dad shouts something down, strained and urgent, and now she follows him up. For a minute I stand in the kitchen, keeping still and silent, my heart pounding as I try to listen. My body tenses as my eyes drift to the marble run that is scattered on the table from our practice and I quickly start to put it away, tidying the table, washing our glasses and putting them in the cupboard. I don't know why but I close the window and check the back door is locked. Then Grandmother comes back in.

"Good boy," she says quietly. "Now hurry. You must go and pack a few things."

"Why? Are we going somewhere? Is Dad OK?"

She nods slightly, but I can see the fear in her eyes. "He will be down in a minute. You need to be ready."

I say I will, but I am too slow to move and she pushes me roughly. "Go!" she shouts urgently, ripping the air. She shoves me out of the room, shocking me with her strength. "One bag," she insists. "As fast as you can."

I race upstairs and stare around my room. How do you pack just one bag? I grab my rucksack and shove some underwear and a couple of clean T-shirts into it. My other pair of jeans, my phone charger and a few old photos. I forget socks and my toothbrush and anything to sleep in. I forget anything in case the weather gets cold. And then Dad is at the door.

"I have to go," he says.

His hair is a mess and his eyes are wild. He stares at me like he doesn't know what to say.

"Dad, what's happened?" I ask, and he hesitates for a moment, then seems to decide. He sits down on the bed and pulls me down next to him.

"I'm doing what I can, Alex," he says. "I've been taking documents from the post office. Documents that prove what's happening here; about what they're doing. About the orders that are being sent around. I took them so I can show people, but they found out this morning. And I need to leave."

"How come you weren't arrested?"

He hesitates again and I can see the fear in his eyes. "They don't know it was me," he says. "But it won't take them long to find out." He shakes his head and sounds sad, like he's forgotten how to be happy. "If I go now I can maybe leave the country tonight."

"What if—" I start, but then I stop myself and take a deep breath. "It's not going to get better is it?" I say.

He shakes his head. "No. But you must stay here and look after your grandmother. I will try to call you when I get to England."

He hesitates awkwardly then holds out his hand for me to shake but I have my hand tangled in the straps of my bag and it takes me a moment. He frowns when he sees the bag.

"What's that?" he says.

"Grandmother told me to pack a bag," I say. "I think she was confused."

His face clouds and he stands up quickly, calling out to Grandmother. He leaves the room and I follow him down the stairs into the hallway.

"Did you tell him to pack a bag?" he snaps angrily.

"He's going with you," she says, then her hand shoots up to stop him arguing. She is staring at the phone.

And it starts ringing.

I am at the top of the stairs, staring down, standing with my back against my bedroom door, feeling my heart racing and the panic building inside me.

"Leave it," Dad insists, but she shakes her head.

"Get your things. There isn't long."

He starts to argue, but his voice cuts off abruptly when her hand reaches for the telephone. She picks it up and answers calmly. It's like the room is frozen.

"No, I'm afraid he's at work, Captain," she says. "Can I help?"

There is a pause while I listen to my heartbeat. "I don't think he'll be back for at least another hour," she says. "I'll get him to call you, shall I?"

Dad is straining to say something, but Grandmother turns her back to him. My heart races on.

"If you want to send someone to wait, I'll be

here," she says.

Dad's jaw tenses and he steps forward. "You can't—" he starts, but she just whips her hand over the speaking end of the phone and twists further away. "I'll expect you in –" she pauses – "fifteen minutes. Goodbye, Capt—"

But they have rung off. She stares at the phone in her hand for a moment then turns to Dad. "They'll be here in five," she says. "You both need to be gone in three."

Dad looks stunned. "What are you talking about?" he asks. "Alex can't come with me. It's going to be dangerous. He needs to stay here with you."

But she shakes her head. "He can't stay here with me," she says, and then she takes his face in her hands. "Open your eyes, Sav," she adds gently. "I'm dying. I've got a few months at most and if you ever come back, I will be gone. This way I can buy you some time and you can be together."

Dad shakes his head. "He's just a boy..." he starts, but now Grandmother's voice is angry.

"He's your son!" she shouts at him. "Just as you are mine. Now, you need to get moving."

She starts giving orders, sending me to the kitchen

to pack some food, then talking to Dad about currency. And when Dad doesn't react, she yells at him, telling him to think. She tells him to focus, that the police are on their way, that he doesn't have long. Eventually he seems to snap back into shape and then he rushes up the stairs.

I go back out to the hall. "He doesn't want me to go," I say, but she shakes her head.

"He isn't thinking straight," she says. "Now hurry. There is so little time."

She tells me to put my bag in the car so I dash outside and am just about to open the boot when I stop. The police will know this car. They will look for it and they will find us. It is hundreds of kilometres to the border and we will be stopped well before we make it. They will be watching the train stations and there is no other way. I think about going back and telling Dad, but then I have a better idea. The house next to ours is still empty and in front of it is parked their old blue Skoda. It hasn't moved for two weeks but maybe it will be OK. I just need to find the keys.

I run down the side of their house and jump over the small gate that guards the garden, then break a window to open the door.

I let myself in.

Then I run into the hallway of the house looking for where they might have kept their keys. There is a table in the hall with a drawer, but it just has a notepad and a pencil. I run back into the kitchen and look around. Then I am out of time.

I let myself in.

Then I run into the kitchen, pulling open drawers and cupboards. On the back of a cupboard door is a series of hooks with keys hanging on them. I am out of time.

I let myself in then run to the cupboard and take the keys. Then I race back to the street and open the car, putting the keys in the ignition and turning them. The car turns over slowly, then fires suddenly. I leave the engine running and run back to the house.

When I get back and see Dad hugging Grandmother, it seems so unusual that I hesitate at the doorway. "Maybe we could all go," he starts, but she dismisses it.

"Sav," she whispers. "I can't go anywhere. I am best use to you here if I can delay them."

"They might punish you."

She laughs. "Let them try. I have been through worse."

"Won't you change your mind about Alex?" he asks.

"No," she says. "You're his father. You need each other. Besides," she adds, "he has a few seconds now. He will be able to help."

Dad pulls away, shaking his head. "A few seconds!" he repeats angrily. "A few seconds will be long enough to get us killed and nothing else."

She catches my eye as I linger by the doorway and doesn't respond, just ushers Dad out. She kisses him again but doesn't say goodbye to me and I wonder why, but there is no time for it now. Dad practically hauls me out of the door towards his car until I tell him about the Skoda. He nods quickly and gets in.

"She thinks of everything, doesn't she," he says, and I don't correct him. I just stay quiet because I don't want to be left behind. We pull away quickly and have reached the other end of the street when he slams his foot on the brake. Then he crashes his hands down on the steering wheel and swears.

"I left the passports in the drawer in my room," he says. "We will need them. We have to go back."

He swerves to the side of the road, then opens his

door, but I just know the police car is going to come round the corner in the next half-second so I scream at him to wait. He pulls his head down so it is out of sight, just as the police car drives past.

"I'll go," I say. "They're not looking for me. They won't even notice."

I don't wait for him to argue, just duck out of the car and stay low, letting the parked cars hide me as I run along. As the two men reach the door I can see one is a large man with a shaved head, blue eyes and a neat blond moustache, wearing a smart uniform. The other man is clearly more junior and stands behind him but I can't see his face. Grandmother opens the door and smiles.

"I am Captain Ivanov," the man with the shaved head says. "This is Corporal Tritzin."

"Welcome, gentlemen," Grandmother says. "But I'm afraid he is not back yet."

Her voice is friendly, but I can see the whites of her knuckles as she grips the doorframe. Her eyes take them in, then look past them for a moment, meeting my gaze, but she shows no sign of recognition. The men are polite but firm. She suggests that as it is a beautiful day perhaps they should wait in the garden.

She could get them a cold beer, she says. She is sure Sav will only be a few minutes.

Ivanov agrees and I crouch down behind the white police car as the soldier turns to look down the street before stepping inside. They walk through the house and I hear the back door open as they go outside. Grandmother is chatting all the time. And she doesn't quite close the front door.

I dart into the hall then up the stairs, trying to keep my step light, urging my heart to stop pounding. In Dad's room is a small dressing table with the passports in the drawer. I open it quickly and silently, then creep back down the stairs, just as the door to the kitchen opens. Corporal Tritzin is standing staring at me. He has dark hair and fierce grey eyes. His nose has been broken in the past and there is a scar on his chin. He sees the passports in my hand and reaches for the gun in the holster on his belt.

I dart up to the house, into the hall then up the stairs, trying to keep my step light, urging my heart to stop pounding. In Dad's room is a small dressing table with the passports in the drawer. I open it quickly and silently, then wait on the landing, listening as the kitchen door opens.

Then Grandmother is there again. "There you are," she says. "If you want to look around, feel free. I have your beer here and there is a bottle opener in the kitchen. What a beautiful day it is."

Corporal Tritzin hesitates, then seems to give in and turns to follow her back out of the hall. She shuts the kitchen door behind them and I creep down the stairs.

As I open the front door, the kitchen door swings open again, as if by accident, and I see Grandmother's back as she talks to one of the men on the other side of the room. She pushes her hand through the gap and waves it to me, until I take the earrings and the necklace from her warm fingers. Then she turns for the briefest moment and smiles at me. There is colour in her cheeks but her eyes are dry. She smiles at me and locks her eyes on mine, as she does when she wants me to practise.

Ignoring the men behind her, she rushes forward and hugs me. She pulls me in tight and I feel the hot tears on my neck. "Remember everything you can," she whispers. "Take the time to practise." The men behind are shouting now, but I ignore them too and promise her I will. Then she tells me to look after myself and my dad. And my time is up.

She smiles briefly, then turns back to the soldiers, closing the kitchen door. And I run out of the house, back to the car, where Dad is waiting. He grunts when I put the passports in his lap and pulls away quickly.

At the end of the road, we turn left, away from the town. Away from the school and the post office and the police station and the barracks. Away from the houses and the church and the train tracks and the friends who were friends and the friends who weren't. Away from everything except memories. I stare out of the rear window of the car as we speed along and the dust flies up.

Knowing I will never see my grandmother again.

8

AFTER

I point the gun and fire. A noise like the earth shattering rips through the air. Rachel's face crumples with shock as the bullet goes past her head. She jerks backwards as her body flinches in horror, crashing into the desk, trying to scramble away, still believing that she is going to die. The room is still for a moment then all hell breaks loose. Max backs into the wall, his hands rising in surrender. Shades is reaching for his belt while Ronnie is yelling at me in words I can't hear.

Then a loudhailer screams from outside.

"ARMED POLICE. EVERYBODY ON THE FLOOR NOW."

Twenty-one seconds have gone past.

My brain feels like it's melting. Ronnie is staring at me. They all are. I must have said something because I haven't moved. I get up, holding Ronnie's eyes firmly with my gaze.

"There's something wrong," I say. "We need to get out now."

Shades is on his feet, angry, not knowing what's going on but mad at me. Ronnie yells at him to keep still. Then he turns and screams at Max to shut up and put his hands up. He pulls the gun out of the drawer and points it at Rachel.

"You too," he says, then he turns to me.

"You sure?" he says.

Shades barks at him, something about dealing with this kid, but Ronnie ignores him.

I turn to Rachel and try to keep my voice calm. "Are you police?" I say.

"Of course I'm not," she says, and she turns and stares at Ronnie. "Who's the kid, Ron? He's going to blow this whole thing."

"She is," I say. "She's police. We need to get out of here."

And now Rachel looks scared. She's got her hands up and there's a gun in her face. She knows the truth and I can see it in her eyes. Ronnie holds the gun steady.

A loudhailer screams from outside.

"ARMED POLICE. EVERYBODY ON THE FLOOR NOW!"

I look at Rachel. She looks scared. She's got her hands up and there's a gun in her face. She knows the truth and I can see it in her eyes.

A look of sadness and fear and desperation. Like a boy with mud on his shirt in a circle of noise. And I can't give her away.

"She's telling the truth," I say. "But there's something

wrong. I heard voices outside."

Ronnie keeps the gun pointed at Rachel and Max. "If anything happens, I shoot you," he says, then he bangs on the door twice. Gold Tooth comes in, looking like he's been dreaming.

"Anything going on out there?" Ronnie says.

Gold Tooth shakes his head. "Just a few workmen," he says.

"How many?" barks Ronnie. He shouts at Shades to pack up and urgently shoves everything back in the bag. "How many?" he yells again at Gold Tooth.

"Five or six," says Gold Tooth. "What's going on?"

"We're out. Go and move the car," says Ronnie. "We'll take the stuff out the back way." He points at Rachel. "Go out the front," he says. "And you try anything, I kill you."

Rachel suddenly gets her voice back.

"What the hell is going on, Ronnie?" she spits. "You busting our deal for some kid? I've got money to make here. People expecting to get paid."

Ronnie doesn't stop moving. He pushes to the back of the office where there is another door behind a curtain and forces it open.

"He says there's people outside and then we find

out there are," he says. "He says you're clean and maybe he's right about that too. But we go now and I make some calls, then we come back to play another time. Got it?"

Max pushes the front door open and strides out. Rachel shoves the envelope back inside her jacket. She glances at me briefly, holding my gaze with an intensity that sends a chill through me. Then the moment has gone and she turns and follows Max. We get outside and walk through the busted cars, old radiators and all kinds of old metal to the wire fence, where Ronnie finds a cut section and squeezes through. The fence backs on to a wide park where kids are playing and old men are walking dogs. We cross the park then make our way down a quiet street until Gold Tooth pulls up in the BMW.

We get in but Ronnie stops Shades. "Give it an hour then go back and clean up in there," he says. "Do it quickly and make sure everything's safe. Then get out."

The car pulls away and Ronnie is on his phone. Barking at someone, accusing them of a million things until he eventually calms down and stares at the road, biting his nails. Gold Tooth doesn't speak.

The world blurs by and I gaze out of the window, the only thought in my mind the look of fear in Rachel's eyes. Like a blind man on the edge of a cliff. Not knowing where the next step might lead. She knows I know who she is but she doesn't know how, and I can almost hear the uncertainty thumping in her chest.

She is alone and surrounded by people she can't trust.

And I wonder if she is just like me.

There is silence most of the way back to the estate. Gold Tooth starts to speak but Ronnie barks at him to "close it" and just sits there chewing at his fingers. But when I put my hand out to open the door, Ronnie tells me to wait.

A few people stare as the car idles but the estate is mostly empty. A kid messes on his skateboard, lonely as rock, up and across, over and over, but he doesn't look up. The sky is gloomy through the dark glass and it feels like the end of the day, although the clock on the dash says it's mid-afternoon. Ronnie tells Gold Tooth to give him a phone then get out of the car. He holds out the phone out to me and I stretch to take it, but he doesn't let go.

"How the hell do you do it?" he says quietly.

There is fear in his eyes and I sit there staring at him, with a gift that feels like a curse and the world melting around me.

"I don't know," I say. "My grandmother showed me. It is hard to explain."

He scratches at his chest absent-mindedly and the dragon peeps out at me, eyes and fire. From somewhere I feel it is a warning not to say more.

He nods and lets me take the phone. "The police are getting closer." He chews at a finger on his left hand for a moment. "You don't like the police, do you, Little Bear?"

"No, Ronnie," I say.

He leans across and opens the door but I don't get out.

"Well?" he says.

"You need to pay me," I say. "I need money to find my dad."

He grunts as if he had forgotten. Then he smiles with thin lips and narrow eyes. "Little Bear gets fed while the rest go hungry, right?"

I hold his gaze. "You promised," I say. "You wanted what I can do and you need to pay me for it."

He pulls a wad of cash out his pocket and peels off a twenty-pound note.

"We said a hundred," I say. "I need this to last until I see my dad. You said it could be a week."

"I didn't get paid so you don't get paid," he says. "You can sleep on the beach, but don't get picked up."

I reach out and take the note. "Don't worry about me," I say. "I can survive."

He shrugs. "There could be more work if you want it."

I swing the door open. "Maybe," I say. "But only until I find my dad and get those documents so we can stay. Then after that I won't need to work for you again."

But Ronnie just finds this funny. He laughs, genuinely, then leans back in the seat, tipping his head back and running his hands through his short hair. "You want to go to school, do you?" he says. "You want to learn how to be a gentleman and get a job as a stockbroker and live on the village green eating roast beef on Sundays?" He puffs out his cheeks and shakes his head. "What a world this is."

He goes on. "We all had dreams. We all want a TV life and a big car and a magic door that opens to the world we were promised. And maybe some people get it," he adds. "Maybe if you have a gift or luck or money or something you can have it."

He turns to me and there is a sadness in his eyes that fills the afternoon. "But Baba Yaga ends up in the fire, Little Bear. And there is always another man to pay. We are from a place no one cares about. So no one cares about us.

"It's the way of the world."

9

BEFORE

I lurch awake in the dark. Yellow light from the street lamps strobes into the car, but we are going slower now. Both lanes are full of traffic and large, illuminated signs above the carriageways scream down their orders. I check the time. It is half past one in the morning.

"Are we at the border?" I ask.

Dad grunts. "Yeah."

"Do you have a plan?"

His face twists. "Kind of," he says.

"Kind of? Will they be looking for us here?"

He nods. "My name will be in the system by now." He turns to me briefly, a grim look on his face. "We also need to ditch the car."

I guess before it had seemed something like an adventure, but now suddenly the impossibility of what we are trying to do is real. There is a small rest area up ahead and Dad pulls into it and parks. He twists in his seat to face me.

"You need to do exactly what I tell you, OK?" he says. "Exactly," he repeats. "Because if you don't we'll be caught and—"

"I might be able to help," I say, but he reacts angrily.

"None of that," he snaps. "I need to know I can trust you, OK?"

If that's how he wants it that's fine, I think. "What happens if they catch us?" I ask.

He looks away for a moment. "They will send me to a prison camp," he says, then he hesitates. "You must say I forced you to come. Then go back home. There are people who will help."

In the thin light that spills in from passing headlights Dad's face looks black and sombre. "You could still go back now," he says. "They are not looking for you."

But I shake my head. "I want to stay."

He nods and turns away. "OK," he says. "From now on we speak only English. We wait for a coach of tourists to stop. Then we get on it."

It doesn't seem like much of a plan but I don't know any different. He parks in the far corner of the car park and we sit there with the lights off, watching the stream of traffic come in and out to use the bathroom facilities. It is mostly small cars and the occasional lorry. A coach pulls in and we get out and walk to the restroom, but as we mingle with the passengers, Dad shakes his head and we slip back into the shadows and wait. A while later, another coach pulls in and this time Dad is more positive, standing by the side of the bus until it is ready to leave. He pretends to talk on his phone in English while I linger by a large sign a few metres away, but again, as the people get back on the bus, we are left behind.

By the time the third coach arrives it is three in the morning and the passengers on board are clearly tired and stiff from travelling. Most of them get off to use the facilities or to stretch their legs, and various European and American voices swirl around me. I study the sign of rules like before: the list of countries that must offer biometric data on entry, the validity of documents issued in the militarised zone, a list of goods that may not be brought in and out of the country. Then, somewhere in the background, I eventually hear what we have been waiting for.

"Driver," one of the old guys is saying in an American accent. "I've left my passport in my case. Could you open up so I can get it out?"

The driver shakes his head and pretends not to understand, but the guy doesn't let up. I see Dad tense and turn towards me. "It's in my bag," the man says. "I'm gonna need it to get through. I know it's a pain, but..."

He's about sixty, dressed in a grey sweater and jeans, with a New York Yankees baseball cap on his head. Then a woman the same age, with long fair hair and a Dolce & Gabbana sweatshirt, walks up and gives the driver a ten-dollar note, which he looks at and stuffs into his pocket. He takes his keys and opens up the luggage hold along the bottom of the coach. Dad nods once, and I walk over to him. The American points to the front of the bus so we move to the rear; me in front of Dad, hidden by him as he talks into his phone in English, pretending to be trying to sort out a visa.

The driver has to take out some bags before he gets to the American's. Dad takes his phone away from his ear. "Call me now," he hisses. "Withhold your number." Then he turns and walks casually past the front of the coach.

I do it and after a few seconds I hear his phone ringing from inside the luggage hold where he has thrown it.

The driver has retrieved the man's bag and now turns to see where the ringing is coming from. He finds the phone and I disconnect just as he picks it up and stares at it. He holds it above his head.

"Has anyone lost a phone?" he says in broken English. "Whose phone is this?" But nobody claims it. He asks the people around him and one of them repeats it in French, while the driver goes back on to the bus to ask the passengers on board, but of course there is no response. I hear him shout out again, then he gives up and starts closing the hold doors. Dad and I lie still, curled up in the gaps between the suitcases as the doors slam. And the world goes dark.

I lie still, staring into the blackness while the coach drives off. Dad rolls over some of the bags until he is near the front, then I hear him rustling about. The bus drives pretty fast for a while, then slows. Then it crawls forward, stopping and starting for what seems like hours, until finally the brakes go on again and we hear the hiss of the doors opening. Then Dad is by my side, pushing me down towards the back of the bus.

"We're at the border," he says. "They're going to open the doors and start taking off the bags so be ready to go. And remember. Speak only English."

As we curl up behind a big blue suitcase right at the back of the coach, I realise I am holding my breath. Slowly I breathe out until I hear the key in the hold lock, then a scrape as the handle turns. I tense, ready to move, just as the coach driver leaps back in surprise.

Dad has opened one of the bags and tied it by its straps to the inside of the hold door so it falls out as soon as soon as the door opens, spilling someone's clothes all over the road. The driver swears and starts picking everything up. The passengers are getting off the bus and crowd around him to help, complaining about how careless he must have been.

And Dad and I slip out at the other end of the bus, without anyone noticing.

We are parked in front of a grey stone building with glass windows through which we can see a number of border guards. They seem bored, staring at screens and talking to each other, in no hurry to process the coach. Lights high above us throw shadows in the night. In a bay next to us another bus has been stopped and a large group of locals are milling around looking bored. We stand at the back of the crowd, pretending to be part of the group, close to the line that divides us from the bus. Nobody talks much. Even the tourists seem pretty nervous about being here. I freeze as someone from our coach looks at me for a minute, but then she looks away. Nobody wants to cause a problem.

At the front of the coach, two officials stand holding a big pile of passports and counting the passengers getting off. When the last tourist steps down, the first official finishes the count and passes the documents to her colleague. She then looks over the luggage that has been left on the side, picking out two pieces and calling forward the owners. A young German guy with glasses steps forward and then one of the Americans. The officials pick their passports out of the pile and tell them to take their bags inside for a customs check. Neither of them understands what is happening and the young guy in particular looks scared. I have this mad urge to go and explain to him, but I can't. I just watch on with the others while he goes into the building and then we wait for what seems like hours but is probably minutes. The Americans complain, but only to each other and not loud enough to be heard. "This is how it works around here," one of them says. He insults my country. I stand at the back, trying not to be noticed.

Eventually the two guys come back and we are told we are OK to go through. Several passengers head back to the bus and Dad edges towards the luggage compartment. I guess he is thinking about a way to get back into the hold, but he has got things wrong. The guard waves and shouts at the passengers to stay away from the bus. We go through on foot, he says. The bus goes through separately.

Suddenly I see the panic in Dad's eyes. Everyone is told to get their luggage and walk it through the border control while the bus is checked and then driven through. Nobody understands but they seem to work it out and get in a line with their bags. We sling our bags over our shoulders and slide into the line to pass through a metal detector, and now I can feel the tension rising inside me. Beyond the guard, on the other side of the detector, is Europe. But they are counting the passengers once more, and the guard is going to notice if there are too many.

Dad tries not to show it, but I notice him turning and looking around. We are towards the end of the queue, edging closer to the front between a French group and two Americans. I can tell Dad is thinking about running, but there is nowhere to run to. People drop their metal objects into a box then pass through the metal detector and I watch as the guard's lips move as he counts the tourists. Dad's hand is clamped on my shoulder. We take another step forward and I feel him tense.

"Act confident. Then when we get to the front, we run," Dad whispers. "Are you ready?"

I turn sharply towards him, watching as he tries to hide the panic in his eyes and the strain on his face. We will be caught if we run and it seems crazy. There must be a better way.

I stare at the guard with the passports, watching his lips move silently as he counts us through, watching as he rolls his shoulders after a long night's work. He waits as the alarm beeps and a man is sent back through to empty his pockets once more. The guard rubs his face and I see the gold of his necklace, the grey of the stubble on the underside of his chin and the blue of the tattoo peeping out from under his sleeve. I need to use my seconds.

There are just eight people left to go through. Four French, me and Dad, and the American couple behind us. The guard beckons another through and I watch as his lips move slightly as the woman passes through without a problem. As her husband strides forward I step out of the line and walk up to the guard. His eyes flash angrily at me but he doesn't say anything, just holds up his hand while the man walks through and mouths the words "thirty-eight". Then he spins to face me. "What the hell do you want?" he barks...

If I go after Dad I will be number forty-two. I laugh loudly and slap Dad on the back. "He has a football tattoo," I whisper. "Talk about the Champions League." And then I laugh again.

"It will be an English club," I say in English. "The Premier League is too strong. Even Barcelona and Real Madrid can't compete."

Maybe Dad wonders how I know about the tattoo but I guess he thinks this is my way of seeming casual and he accepts it. The last French woman goes through and Dad forces out a comment in English. "You can't write off the Spanish teams," he says clumsily. "And what about the Germans?"

"Bayern Munich!" I look at the guard and roll my eyes. The woman steps clear and Dad moves forward. I wait for the guard's lips to mouth the next number then I say "thirty-eight" firmly in our language. I want to confuse him; to put the wrong number in his head, but as soon as I speak his eyes flick up towards me. I smile as if I am still talking about the football and

turn quickly back to Dad. "Half their team are injured,"
I say. "They haven't got a chance."

Dad stares at me for a moment, not sure if I have
said anything, then he goes on turning to look at
me as he passes through the detector. "What about
Juventus?" he says.

"Juventus can't score goals," I say, watching the
slightly confused expression on the guard's face.
"Thirty-nine," I say, looking away for a moment.

And then I go through.

I walk forward to where Dad is standing a metre
away, not knowing if I have done enough to confuse
the count, but ready to run if necessary. Dad watches
me and I see him shuffle his bag over his shoulder
ready to sprint. As I reach him he turns and mouths
the word "ready", but I shake my head. I just want to
wait a little longer to see if it worked.

Dad's face creases with frustration but I ignore
it and watch the guard as he counts the last two
through. I feel Dad's hand on my shoulder, squeezing
my jacket to pull me forward just as a flicker of doubt
passes across the guard's face. My heart is pounding
and Dad's arm is round my shoulders, urgently trying
to turn me away but I ignore him. The exit is twenty

metres away, with more officers on either side, and running is never going to work. The guard is in front of me, looking confused. For a moment he stands there as if working out what to say. Then he shakes his head and shrugs.

"It is wrong," he says in half-formed English. "Champions League is Liverpool."

And he smiles and tucks his papers under his arm, then walks back into the building. The gate at the end of the compound is open and we are waved through to a car park to wait for the coach. The tourists mill about but we ignore them and keep walking towards a sign for buses, where we wait at a deserted bus stop. As the sun rises behind us, I finally feel my heart rate slow down. We've made it and the relief floods through me. Until Dad turns to me with a face full of fury.

"You did something, didn't you?" he hisses. "What the hell were you thinking, taking risks like that? You promised you would do exactly what I said and at the first opportunity you go using your tricks."

His voice is low but angry and his eyes are almost burning. "Don't you realise what would happen to me if I am caught?" he says. "How can we make this journey if I can't trust you?"

And all the relief of a few moments ago evaporates like steam in a desert.

"It worked, though..." I start, but Dad doesn't care.

"I need to know you're on my side, Alex," he says coldly. "I am fighting too many battles to fight you too." Then he sits back with his arms crossed.

I feel like I've been slapped. I know he's scared and I know he's got to look after me, which he wasn't expecting, but I don't feel like he's given me a chance. Maybe he's right, I think. Maybe I shouldn't do anything without telling him first but there didn't seem to be any time.

"I'm sorry," I mumble, and he looks away.

"That's all right," he says eventually, like he feels he has to say something. Then we wait in silence.

After a while the bus comes and we get on and Dad buys tickets with a currency I did not know he had, and then we go and sit at the back.

And suddenly I feel as lost as I have ever felt.

10

AFTER

I've got twenty pounds, a phone and nothing else so I wander around until I find a free Wi-Fi signal at a coffee shop then look for news about last night, but there doesn't seem to be much to learn. Border patrols intercepted a boatload of illegal immigrants just off the UK coast. Detainees are being held near Gatwick, waiting to be processed, but after all that's happened, I don't even know if Dad made it on to the boat. I check my phone for messages but there's nothing. If he made it across he'll meet me at the post office on Monday. If they caught him I'll have to wait until they process him before I can see him. If he didn't get across, he'll get me a message.

The alternative doesn't bear thinking about.

I wander back to the estate, where there's a fish and chip shop, and I add my voice to the babble in the queue, then pay for the chips with the twenty-pound note. I have nowhere to go so I start walking slowly down to the beach. I'm just trying to figure out what I do next when a blue Astra roars up behind me.

I burst into a run as its tyres hit the kerb and the ton of metal screeches up towards me. I jerk to the side, then sprint off again, but the car swerves in front of me so I can't get past.

"Get in," shouts the driver, and I turn to see Rachel. There is urgency in her eyes and panic in her voice. Heads are turning.

"Get in," she shouts again, even as I'm backing off, but she reverses, slewing the car round so she almost hits me. "For God's sake," she yells. "Get in the bloody car before anyone sees you. Do it now!"

She leans over and pushes the door open. "You need to trust me," she says. "We know about Ronnie and we've been watching this estate. We could have had the whole place pulled apart if we'd wanted to but we didn't. You think we're interested in a kid like you? Unless you want every officer in Sussex down here in five minutes, you'll get in the bloody car."

When she says that, about watching, I feel the blood drain from my body. Her face is flushed and I notice her knuckles are white on the steering wheel.

I open the door. I check the handle from the inside to see if it will open. I look and see that she has her seatbelt on and wouldn't be able to move quickly. I get in and we pull away.

"Are you going to arrest me?"

"How did you know I was a police officer?"

"You were there to catch them, weren't you? Why

didn't you?"

*She laughs without humour. "If we'd wanted
Ronnie we could have had him months ago." Then her
face turns serious. "Now listen, kid. You need to tell
me how you knew because at the moment it's just
me, but in five minutes it will be the drug squad, the
immigration department and everybody else I can
call. You saved my life today but I need to know how
you..."*

*She must see my face when she says "immigration".
"Is that what you're scared of?" she says. We are at
the bottom of the road with the sea in front of us. She
turns left then left again, up one of the side streets.
Then she stops.*

"OK, kid," she says. "Let's talk."

I don't see any danger so I let it play.

"OK, kid," she says. "Let's talk."

"I won't let you arrest me."

The words come out automatically. Rachel stares
at me for a moment and then her face softens. I
notice the dark lines under her grey eyes and the
slight freckles on her cheeks. She wears no make-
up and I can see the tiny white cracks in her lips. She
sighs.

"What's your name?"

"Aleksander."

"How old are you?" she says.

"Fourteen."

"Who are you here with?"

"My dad," I say. "He will be here soon."

I can tell she doesn't believe me. There is silence for a moment. Then she turns off the ignition.

"We need to get out of the car," she says.

"Why?" I say. "Have I said something wrong?"

She shakes her head. "No," she says. "But I've just had this car cleaned and your chips stink."

It takes me a moment to realise it's a joke because it seems out of place. She smiles at me and I try to smile back, but it's hard.

"It's just English humour," she says. "You'll get used to it pretty soon."

But I don't know if she's right.

We find a bench overlooking the sea and sit down watching the wind turbines turn slowly on the horizon. I remember what Grandmother said about sharing and ask if she would like some chips. She smiles and takes one then tells me I will do well in this country because I like my chips covered in vinegar. I tell her I will do well because I will work harder than anyone else.

"You speak good English," she says. "Want to tell me where you're from?"

I shake my head.

"That's OK," she says. "I can guess. Your name, your accent..."

I change the subject. "Why don't you arrest Ronnie? They have guns. They must be bad."

She asks me how long I've known him. I tell her not long.

She sighs and twists on the bench so she can see me properly. She looks at me for a long time, just thinking, until eventually she seems to make up her mind.

"Are we going to be straight with each other?" she says. "I want to know how you knew I was a police officer. There was a minute today when I thought my time had come, but you didn't tell them. I need to know what's going on before I walk into another room like that again."

I don't know what to say so I don't answer.

I take one of the last chips from the paper in front of us and she watches me eating it. "When did you last eat something healthy?" she says. Then she looks at me as if she is peeling the grime on my skin back with her eyes. "When did you last change your clothes?"

"There's people a lot worse than me," I say.

She takes the empty paper and screws it up, throwing it into the bin next to us. "Maybe," she says. "But I bet you never thought it would be like this, did you?"

I shake my head.

"The things I've seen," she says. "When did you come over?"

"Yesterday."

"Have you got any money?"

"Some," I say.

"Why did your dad leave you with Ronnie?"

I don't answer and she looks across sharply. "Where is your dad?"

"I don't know," I say.

It is getting cooler and I cross my arms in front of my chest. In the distance, the sea has turned pink as the sun falls. The lonely voices of seagulls scream in the sky.

"You were on that boat yesterday, weren't you?" she says. "They thought they picked everyone up. I guess maybe they didn't."

I shrug again. "I guess not."

"Got anywhere to stay?" she asks.

I don't know what to say, because I haven't. I've no idea what I'm going to do.

"I've got some money," I say. "I'll be OK."

She leans back, staring at the horizon. "As long as you don't have to rescue any more useless policewomen on the way?"

I look up at her, surprised at her words and the nervousness on her face.

"This is the point when you're supposed to say, 'You weren't useless, just unlucky,'" she says, and I guess she thinks she screwed up somehow. But she didn't.

"You were unlucky," I say. And I smile because it's true.

She watches me for a moment then smiles back, her face relaxing for the first time.

"I can find you somewhere to stay," she says. "There are places that will look after you."

I shake my head. "They will lock me up."

"Don't you want to claim asylum? Isn't that why you're here?"

I shrug. "I need to wait for my dad. I'm going to meet him at nine a.m. tomorrow in London. He needs to get some documents from a post office that will help us. Then we can hand ourselves in."

Rachel pulls a face. "You shouldn't spend the night on the street," she says. "But if you won't give yourself up there aren't many alternatives."

The seagulls circle above us, their forlorn cries tearing the air as they guard their territory. Rachel drums her fingers on the arm of the bench as she thinks hard.

"Have you ever done anything bad, Aleksander?"

I shake my head and wonder what she means. She is dealing with men with guns and passports and gold and maybe whatever I do compared to that is like a grasshopper chirping in the wind. "No," I say. "I don't think so."

She hesitates, then seems to make up her mind. "You saved my life today so maybe I have a chance to help you in return," she says. "I know people in immigration and I know the system. If you answer a few questions I'll help you get your documents and find your dad."

She gets up and walks back to the car, opening the

94

passenger door then walking round to the driver's side. Then she leans on crossed arms across the roof of the car as I stand next to the open door and wait for the catch.

"But I won't do it unless I know you're somewhere safe and away from Ronnie. If you won't go to a hostel I can only think of one other place," she says. "Get in the car. You'll have to come home with me."

11

BEFORE

We get off the bus at the end of the line. Dad seems to know where he's going but I can feel the tension radiating off him so I don't ask too much. We stop at a large department store, where I trail along behind him to the desk that sells mobile phones, then watch while he buys a new mobile and a blank SIM card with cash. Then we leave and walk south, past shops interspersed with seedy offices that gradually turn into run-down convenience stores, metal-working plants and engine-repair units. As we keep walking I can sense people watching us and I wonder how different we look. Our clothes seem old-fashioned, our bags look heavy, our eyes are cast down. Already we do not belong.

Eventually we reach a wide stretch of tarmac covered with old cars, scattered randomly like a rash on skin. Behind them there is an old shipping container that has had the front cut out to become a makeshift office, sheltered from the sun by a faded blue awning. Dad talks to one of the men there for a few minutes, then we are taken to see an old Nissan that looks like it is more rust than metal. I don't know much about cars, but I watch as Dad checks the vehicle identification number on the windscreen to the framework under the bonnet, then pulls back the carpet in the footwells to make sure the car hasn't been stitched together from two wrecks. The tyres are pretty bald, but when he starts the engine it sounds healthy enough. It's got to get us 1,700 kilometres across to France and then it can fall apart, but Dad seems to check it as carefully as he can. Then he gives the guy five hundred US dollars in cash.

Twenty minutes later we are on our way.

It takes an hour of driving without the car falling apart or the sound of sirens and flashing lights in the mirrors before I feel like I can breathe normally. Dad seems to sense it and he looks up but doesn't say anything before his eyes move back to the front. Around us, heavy traffic weaves and glides on a wide road and I feel hidden in the anonymous blue car. We are heading for the middle of Europe and it seems like we are a grain of sand in the desert. We should be safe. At least for a little while.

Dad has dumped his jacket on the back seat and he tells me to get the new phone out of it and store the number. As I take it out of his pocket some papers spill on to the floor so I scramble into the back, only realising they are photographs when I pick them up. There is an old one of Dad as a boy; one of Grandmother with my grandfather, who I never met; a big group of Dad's friends from when he was younger; one of a pretty young woman holding a baby.

Then I turn over the last one and my heart seems to stop beating as the memories flood back.

It is me, the little bear. Big, dark brown eyes peering out from a cheeky face, with a secret I didn't even know myself yet. My neck is scrunched into a green knitted sweater and there is a narrow little smile on my face. Unruly blond hair falls over pink skin, and in front of me one small hand is bunched into a fist.

I am looking up at the camera, over the top of several playing cards held in my other hand. Grandmother is sitting across the table, twisting to glare with frustration at the camera lens. White hair tied back in a scarf, sparkling green eyes piercing through wrinkles, long mottled fingers always holding aces and kings. Or jokers sometimes. In the background, reflected in the glass of the window, my mother stands as still as a ghost. Hands clasped in front of her body, in a long dark dress but with no expression in the refracted light. Tall and stern and almost forgotten, she watches while my father laughs and tries to get the hang of the camera.

"No more photos, Sav," my grandmother orders. "We are trying to play a game." She turns back towards me and leans forward. "Now then, Little Bear," she says quietly. "Let's try again."

I lean forward and she puts the cards back into two piles, in front of us. Then she picks one up and puts it down face up. I pick one up and put it down, hardly looking at it. She picks one up and her hand hovers over the pile.

"Snap!" I say, laughing. "Give the cards to me."

Grandmother hesitates. The jack of diamonds is still in her hand, half turned up, and she looks at it for a moment before smiling and gathering the cards. We pick up our piles again and this time it is eight rounds before I take one off the top of my pile.

"Snap!" I squeal.

Grandmother puts on her outraged face. "You didn't show it to me," she says. "How can I compete if you don't show me the cards?"

"I'm not cheating, Babusya," I say. "I wasn't looking."

She nods, but this time there is a question in her eyes. "Let's play again," she says, "but this time I will just turn over all the cards and you say snap as quickly as you can."

I grin because this is a game I am good at. She takes the whole deck and turns over the cards one by one into two piles.

"Snap!" I say, and she nods.

"Faster, Little Bear," she says. "Faster."

And the next time I am faster. She keeps dealing and I am always right. Always as fast as I can. Faster than ever. Faster than her fingers will turn. She peels the cards and throws them down and I call out louder and louder, like a merry-go-round, whirring and spinning and shrieking with laughter.

"Snap!" I yell as her fingers close on one of the last cards, but then she doesn't throw it down. And there is something wrong, because there is an ace on the table, but she hasn't put down the card in her hand. She leans back in her chair and fixes me with a gaze as slow as time itself. Behind her, Dad is watching. And Mum looks scared.

The card falls from her fingers. It is the ace of diamonds, just like I knew it would be.

"It seems we are blessed," she says softly. "My little bear has a gift."

Dad looks shocked. Like something has happened that he has been dreading. He turns slightly pale and looks at Grandmother, who nods, once, quickly. Then he sits down heavily and stares at me before responding to something my mother whispers with a helpless shrug. I look up at her and slowly my body seems to freeze. She is staring at me with a look on her face like I have never seen before. Her hard, grey eyes are wide and she is breathing fast. She says something too quickly for me to catch, then moves her fingers from her forehead to her chest to both her shoulders.

I remember wondering why they didn't look happy, because Grandmother said I had a gift and I thought they would be pleased, but Dad looks sad and Mum looks angry. And lost, and something I don't understand. Then she turns and leaves the room.

That night there was shouting. And I never saw my mother again.

12

AFTER

I don't know why I agree to go with Rachel. Maybe because I have nowhere else to go. Maybe it is because I need her to keep her promise. Maybe it's because I looked into her eyes when she thought she was going to die, although I guess she doesn't know that. She pulls out, driving fast like she owns the road and within a few minutes we are in the middle of town in a winding row of houses, trying to find a parking space in a road crowded with cars. She hammers into a space about two centimetres longer than the car itself, then gets out quickly, leading me back to a small iron gate that leads down a path to a white plastic front door. She steps through the gate then turns to me.

"This is my home," she says. "And I'm trusting you. Please don't let me down."

We enter into a narrow hallway with faded blue carpet and cream walls. I turn and check the lock and I could get out if I wanted to. In front of me, stairs lead upwards and to my right there is an open door into a living room. Rachel leads the way and I am surprised when she calls out that she's home.

There is a shout from upstairs. A girl's voice. Rachel asks her to come down to meet me. Then she turns to me. "I live with my daughter," she says. "You're in her home too." Then she smiles as a girl appears at the top of the stairs. "This is Hayley," she says. "Hayles, this is Aleksander."

Hayley stops halfway down when she sees me. She looks about my age and is shorter than her mum, with long fair hair piled high on her head and big green eyes behind round, black glasses. She wears faded blue combat jeans and a striped green top and has bare feet and I guess from the pencil stuck between her teeth that she was in the middle of something. She reaches out for the banister and stares at me, taking me in for a moment, unsure of what's going on.

"Who is he?" she says, in a rough voice like Rachel's. Her body tenses when she sees me and I can tell she is strong and athletic. She takes a step down the stairs towards her mum, almost protectively, as she looks at me, weighing me up. Like a fighter watching an opponent.

"Someone who needs our help," Rachel says. "Could you run a bath?"

I don't see it but I guess a look must pass between them as Hayley's expression changes from suspicious to completely blank. She runs back upstairs and a few seconds later I hear the sound of water running. Rachel leads me through into the living room and tells me to sit on a brown sofa while she checks something.

When she leaves the room I am up and at the door. She goes upstairs and as I peer around, I see her turn right at the landing. I crouch down low and listen.

"...be careful," she says. "He seems like a good kid, but I don't know him."

"Why is he here?" Hayley asks.

"It's to do with work," Rachel says. "He showed up and something happened and I think he saved my life. And he's got nowhere else to go."

"Why can't he go to a shelter or something? Why does he have to come here?"

I am out of time.

I count to fifteen.

Then I dart out of the room and up the stairs, crouching low to listen.

"...here illegally. He's got no one and if we put him in the system he'll just run. I need to talk to him about what he knows. A day or so will work for both of us."

"Provided he's not some lunatic."

"You can look after yourself but be careful," Rachel says, and now I can hear her voice turn towards me.

"Fine," says Hayley. "But if anything happens I'm calling..."

I am out of time.

Rachel comes back in and passes me a towel then sends me to the bathroom, where I check the lock on the door then get into the steaming water. It feels like months since I have washed, and under the grime I feel weak and vulnerable. After ten minutes Rachel knocks on the door and tells me she has left some clothes outside. I come out and take them. It is a pair of old black jeans and a large rugby shirt, both splattered with paint, which she said used to belong to Hayley's dad but now she uses for overalls. There is also a pair of socks and underwear that Hayley has borrowed from a friend who lives nearby. The jeans are too big for me but I put them on then come downstairs, clutching my dirty clothes in my arms. Rachel takes them and goes into the kitchen where she says she will wash them. Hayley is sitting on the sofa, just staring at me.

"Feeling better?" Rachel says when she comes back in.

"Thank you," I say, and then I stand there, feeling stupid and weak and ashamed. It's funny that being clean makes me feel more normal. And normal people don't have to beg for somewhere to stay.

Rachel looks at me then suddenly she laughs. "You can sit down, you know," she says. "Move up, Hayles. Let him sit down." Then she adds, "But don't get too comfortable. If you're wearing those clothes you might as well paint the kitchen."

I stare at her, wondering what she is talking about.

"It's a joke," she says. "Don't worry. I'm joking."

Hayley huffs then gets up and stamps across the room to one of the other chairs. "He doesn't get your jokes, Mum," she says. She sits down and gives me a look that suggests this is a total waste of time. "She makes jokes about everything, especially things that aren't funny."

She is about to say something else when there is the buzzing of a phone. Rachel checks the caller, then gets up and leaves the room.

Hayley and I sit staring at each other for a minute before she crosses her arms.

"So what's going on?" she asks.

I hesitate, not knowing what to say. "You know what she does, right?" I manage.

Hayley scowls. "Don't treat me like a kid," she says

aggressively. "I know exactly what she does. She risks her life trying to put away criminals and I accept it." She scowls. "But if you being here makes her life more dangerous than it already is, you'll regret it."

Her eyes are fierce behind her glasses and her chin is set in determination. I believe what she says.

"I know what it is like," I say. "My dad risked a lot—" I break off, not knowing what more to say, but she just sits there, waiting for me to continue. "He tried to do what was right and they came after him. We had to run and then..." I shrug.

Surprise flickers in her eyes and her expression melts a little. "How long have you been here?"

"Since yesterday."

"Is that all?" she says. "Have you registered yet?"

"As what?"

She almost laughs. "For asylum!" she says. "If you're persecuted in your own country there's a good chance you can stay."

"No!" I almost bark out the answer. "We can't tell people who we are," I say. "I need to speak to my dad and see what he says."

"So where's your dad?"

"I haven't seen him since before we crossed. There

was a fight. I was already on board."

She shakes her head. "You need to talk to the authorities. My mum might be able to help. I don't think you have any choice."

They have taken me into their home, but I don't know them and I don't want to talk about this. And I am not going to talk to the authorities before speaking to Dad. I look up and Rachel is watching from the doorway. "You two OK?" she says.

Hayley nods. Rachel looks at me and I nod too.

"Good," she says. "Because we need to talk."

There is a round wooden table in the corner of the room, in front of a second door that leads into the kitchen. It has four chairs round it, although two are covered in papers and magazines and all sorts of clutter. Rachel clears one and I think it is for me to sit down, but instead she moves it away from the wall then gets a knife, which she uses to prise the carpet away from the skirting board. She peels it back then lifts up one of the floorboards beneath it, removing a thick brown card folder, which she then puts on the table.

Then she takes out a number of photos and spreads them out so they are facing me. The first is of Ronnie getting into his car. He is looking away from the camera. On the other side of the BMW are Shades and Gold Tooth, looking like they are arguing about something.

"Romek Andris," she says. "Better known as Ronnie. And in the background are Wayne Mitchell and Brandon Tythe."

She points to the next photo, of Max and a shorter guy I don't recognise.

"Maximilian Gruber and Tomas Black."

"I don't know this guy," I say.

Rachel smiles. "Lucky you," she says. "And if you stay lucky you never will. He was arrested last week and isn't expected home anytime soon. He's the guy whose place I've taken."

She points back to the first picture. "Do you know what your friends are involved in?"

"They are not my friends," I say.

"Do you know what they're involved in?" she repeats.

I'm not stupid and I know it's bad. "They helped us get over from France. We didn't have any other choice."

Hayley scowls, but Rachel reaches out and places a hand on her arm.

"It's OK," she says. Then she leans back in her chair. "One of their sidelines is to sell Max valuables taken from the poor sods who come over from France." She stabs her finger at the photos. "And these are the guys I'm trying to get close to."

Hayley interrupts. "I thought you said this guy Max was dangerous," she says to Rachel. She looks at me. "What were you doing with them?"

But I can't explain, can I?

"I speak different languages," I say. "Ronnie said it would be useful. Today I think he wanted to test me out."

Rachel looks at me and I can see her going through the events of the morning in her head. She frowns a little but doesn't question me.

"And now you can help us," she says. "Ronnie's gang are selling the stuff the people-smugglers take, but they're too small to be running the show. We're trying to find the people who are."

"Can't you just follow them?" Hayley asks. "Find out where they deliver the money to?"

Rachel shakes her head. "We've tried and we didn't get anywhere. We even arrested them all a couple of weeks ago. Made out like it was a drugs bust where we got our information wrong. We searched them but they were all clean, and they acted like they knew we were coming. Ronnie must have passed the stolen goods on to someone we didn't see." She turns to me. "That's where I was hoping you could help."

"Stripes," I say, almost to myself.

"What?"

"Stripes," I say again.

Rachel smiles. "You talking about decorating again or something we can all understand?"

"It was a guy," I say. "We stopped on the way to the meeting. He passed Ronnie the bags of jewellery and a gun. We stopped on the way back too. But it was all too quick. He had a striped T-shirt. That's why I called him Stripes."

Rachel picks up the picture of Ronnie and flicks at the corner of it with her nail absent-mindedly. "Did you get a good look at him?" she asks.

I shake my head. "It all happened really fast. Like it was rehearsed."

"Where did it happen?"

"When he was driving through town. In the lane where there are a lot of people walking in the road. We kept stopping and starting to let the people walk.

I thought it was just another stop until this guy leans in the window. Then it was done."

"Well, it's something," says Rachel. She starts to say more when I yawn. Rachel seems to sit up straight then glances at Hayley before shaking her head.

"I'm so sorry," she says. "It's late and you'll need to catch an early train to London in the morning. You've been a real help."

She gets up and goes upstairs again before coming down with a duvet in a pink cover and a pillow. "You can sleep on the sofa," she says. "You don't mind Hayley's old bedding, do you?"

She gives me a new toothbrush and tells me to use the bathroom while they tidy the living room. As I come back down I hear Rachel tell Hayley to sleep in with her tonight. So she is safe from the strange boy in their house, I think. One who has nowhere else to go.

I lie still in the dark, listening to them moving about until the house is silent. I imagine them together, warm in the blackness, heartbeat to heartbeat, and I try to lie still as if any movement I make would disturb everything. I wish Dad was here. I don't know why I haven't had a message and I don't know what I will do if he isn't at the post office tomorrow. I don't know what I'm going to do for the rest of my life after tonight. I don't understand how this country works or why the people tell the jokes they do or how I could ever have got here.

I lie still in the dark, wishing I could sleep. Because at least that is a place I know.

13

BEFORE

If Dad sees me looking at the photo, he doesn't mention it.

"You're in the way of the mirror," he says. "Get back in the front."

I scramble back over the seats. "Do you think we are safe now?"

Dad hesitates. He looks across at me briefly then looks back at the road ahead. "For a while," he says. "But I don't want to pretend this is going to be easy. And it's too late to turn back." He pauses to overtake an old Mercedes truck then pulls the car back into the right-hand lane. "Some of the things they're doing to people at home are pretty bad," he says. "And they won't want the world knowing. I think they're going to try to stop us passing the documents I took across to anyone."

"Can I see them?"

He shakes his head but smiles at the same time. "I work for the post service and I didn't want to get caught with them. So I sent them to a post office in England where I can collect them." He grins. "Pretty smart, eh?"

I nod. "Pretty smart," I say.

Then his face turns serious again. "The parcel I sent

will be there on Monday morning..." He hesitates.

"What?"

"There are records. They will know that's where it will be. They know we're going to England."

"So you think they'll try and stop us getting there?"

Dad nods. "They'll probably be watching the ports in France and Holland."

"Is there another way?"

"We don't have time to find out. We need to get that parcel at nine o'clock on Monday otherwise they might get it first and that means crossing over tomorrow."

"Even though they'll be watching!"

He stares straight ahead. "I told you it was going to be dangerous," he snaps, but then his voice changes. "I'm sorry," he says. "I know you didn't ask for this either."

"What if we don't get the documents?" I ask.

"Maybe the English won't believe us. Maybe they'll send us back."

"After all this?"

He must hear the tension in my voice because he forces a little lightness into his tone. "Lots of people have got out in the last year," he says. "Maybe they won't bother with us." But he doesn't sound convincing.

"We can't go home though, can we?" I say.

"No."

"Shall I try Grandmother again?"

He nods, but we both know she won't answer. And she doesn't. The phone at the house rings and rings and her mobile goes through to the same voicemail message I have heard ten times already.

There is a long pause. I don't ask the question but I edge closer.

"Grandmother wanted me to practise," I say. "She thinks I can increase the number of seconds I have until it is more useful."

Dad doesn't respond straight away and for a short time I think he might have changed his mind about how useful it was at the border. But after about a minute I realise he is just letting his anger build.

"Your grandmother doesn't realise how much damage that curse can bring," he says bitterly. "It will steal your life away if you let it, and ruin everything you love."

"How?" I start, but I have misjudged things again.

"I don't want to talk about it," he says quietly.

And we drive on in silence.

We drive for hours, following signs for Krakow and Prague, then Dresden. I need to know why Dad thinks my gift is a curse, but the silence in the car is so heavy it's like I'll be crushed if I speak so I just watch the road signs and listen to the music on the car's old radio, interspersed with people talking to us in languages I only half understand. There is a sign that tells us when we pass into Germany, but no real border to cross and we don't slow down.

Dad is in his own world. Sitting staring at the road ahead, gripping the steering wheel hard, leaning forward slightly, like he's angry with me. The road is long and straight, with evenly spaced road signs and I wonder if increasing the time I can take will help persuade him. Grandmother told me to take time to practise and there is something about the monotony of the drive that pulls me towards it. I gaze at the road ahead and hold myself still.

A Mercedes glides past on our outside. A motorbike hovers in front of us, waiting for a gap in the traffic to pull out and roar away. It is forty-five kilometres to Dresden.

I move between the seconds, pulling myself forward and back, concentrating on the road that stretches out in front.

As the signs to the exits flash by, I push myself as far as I can. I get to about twelve seconds, then suddenly our car lurches to the side.

Dad's head jerks up but it is too late. The car crosses the line between the lanes, into the path of a BMW, which hits the wing. Dad overcompensates and swings the steering wheel to the right, but skids into the side of a lorry. The BMW spins and flips up into the air. We hit the lorry and slide along with it for a second before we bounce off its side as if we were a tennis ball. As the air fills with the sound of screeching brakes and bending metal, the car spins until we are facing the wrong way. A Volvo hits us at full speed and my head slams into the window...

I grab Dad's arm and shake him. "Wake up," I say urgently, and he jolts up. His whole body tenses, dragging the wheel slightly to the left and the car swerves across the lanes on the motorway. On our outside, the BMW that was about to overtake us slams on its brakes to avoid us, its horn blaring. The Mercedes behind it isn't paying as much attention and skids behind it, trying to stop, but it can't in time and it thumps into the back of the BMW. A Volvo slows and stops centimetres away from the BMW and all the way behind and around, the traffic slows. As I stare out of the rear window I watch the road grind to a standstill behind us. Dad stares into the mirror for a moment, then looks forward again. He is breathing hard.

"What the hell were you thinking?" he snaps. "You could have killed us."

I start to respond but he holds up his hand to cut me off. "Save it," he says. "I need to stop and get some rest. I'm half asleep. We'll find a hotel at the next services and talk then."

I sit there fuming until the next sign for services where we turn off, sliding quietly into a half-empty car park. Dad books a sparse two-bedded room in the cheaper of the two motels. There is a small restaurant next to the building and he tells me to sit down while he gets us something to eat. He buys me a burger and I wonder how many times in my life I have told him I hate the cheese you get on these things. Dad tries to phone Grandmother but there is still no answer. Somewhere a radio plays music I don't recognise. Outside, darkness falls.

"I saved us," I say.

"What?"

As soon as we speak I see the tension rise in his shoulders and I can feel it in mine too.

"You got angry with me in the car when I saved us," I say. "You were just about to fall asleep and we would have been killed."

Dad drops a French fry back on to his plate and stares at me coldly. "How do you know?"

"Because I was looking ahead. And it's a good job I was because you fell asleep and hit a lorry and we would both be dead."

"You don't know that."

"I do know that," I say. "And you know I do. This ability I've got is amazing, Dad. Grandmother knew it and you're just jealous because you haven't got it when other people in our family have."

The words come out before I can stop them.

Dad waits a moment before he speaks and when he does his words are blunt. "Did you practise that little speech?" he says. "Why don't you tell me how I'm going to respond?"

I shake my head. "Of course not," I say. "But you

need to believe me. I saved us back there."

But Dad shakes his head. "What about the people in the cars behind?" he says. "What if changing things meant someone in one of those cars died or there was an ambulance stopped from getting to hospital because of the hold-up? How do you know whether what you change is for good or bad?"

"I do what I think is right," I say. "Same as for any other decision I make in life. How do you know taking that evidence was the right thing? Don't you think people could suffer because of that? Grandmother, for one."

I don't know why I say it, but the words seem to make him pause. He looks away for a long time and when he turns back there is a pain in his eyes I haven't seen before.

"It's not the same," he says. "And I'm not jealous," he adds. "I could have had the gift but I chose not to."

And now I ask the question that I've wanted to for the last ten hours.

"Did Mum leave because of it?" I ask. "Is that why you hate me?"

"I don't hate you," he says. "I just hate this corruption that our family has. It isn't right to change the future."

"It's not a corruption!" I say. "It's part of me. Like my eyes and my arms and my mind."

But he shakes his head. "It doesn't need to be. You need to work it out before it's too late. Everything in my life went wrong because of that curse. But you'll only understand when you work it out for yourself."

When I don't reply he leans back and closes his eyes for a moment and I wish I could take those words back. Eventually he looks up again. "I shouldn't have married your mother," he says. "Her brother was my best friend and when he died we kind of came together, but we never really loved each other. I think she'd been unhappy for a while and your ability was as good a reason as any for her to leave."

"Didn't she love me?"

"She and her brother were very close," he says. "When he died it was like the love went out of her." He sighs. "She didn't love anyone and it was all because of that curse you call a gift."

He looks like he might say more but he stops himself. "We need to get some sleep," he says. "We've got an early start in the morning."

The conversation is over. We go back to the motel room and go to bed.

14

AFTER

Rachel and Hayley come down together, striding into the living room in a way that's trying not to look too planned. I look at my phone. It is seven o'clock on Monday morning.

"We would have let you sleep," Rachel says, "but if I'd got any hungrier I'd have eaten Hayles."

Hayley is wearing her combat trousers, trainers and a tight T-shirt that shows off her athletic frame and strong arms. Her hair is tied back tight against her head and the glasses have gone. She stands behind Rachel with her arms folded, just staring at me like she expects me to give myself away at any moment. But I don't know what she thinks I might do. Or why I might do it.

"Thanks for letting me..." I start, but Rachel waves my words away. She sends Hayley into the kitchen to make some breakfast then sits down on the sofa next to me.

"Look," she says. "You can't stay here for long. It's not appropriate and it doesn't fit with my job, but we can help you out. I messaged a contact who works for immigration. She says they haven't processed the group you came with yet but as a favour to me she'll go through them and try and find out if your dad was on the boat."

I nod. "Thanks. We said we would meet at the post office. I need to go there in case he escaped like I did."

Hayley appears at the kitchen door with her arms folded. Rachel glances at her then back to me. "I thought you might say that," she says. "So I suggested to Hayles that she could take you up."

I look up to see Hayley staring at me. "You don't mind?" I ask her.

She doesn't answer and I can see that she isn't keen, but I don't know how to get there on my own.

"She's happy to do it," Rachel says in a tone of voice that says Hayley hasn't had any choice. Then she turns back to me. "But tomorrow you hand yourself in," she says. "I know a lawyer who will help you. I'll call her after you get the package, then she will tell you what to do. If we can prove you and your dad are in danger, it will make a big difference. It's as much as I can do. I'm sorry it's not more."

"I don't want to..." I start, but she is up and moving into the kitchen. As she reaches the door, she turns.

"I'm a police officer," she says. "And whatever I owe you, I need to follow the law. There are good people working in these departments. You'll be OK." She smiles a thin, firm smile. "Now I've got to go. Hayley will look after you."

Her eyes lock on Hayley's for a moment and I wonder how much pressure she had to apply to get her to help me. Then Rachel says goodbye and rushes out.

Hayley and I stand in the kitchen in an awkward silence that seems almost unbreakable until I take a slurp of tea and almost spit it out.

"Milk!" I say.

Hayley snorts. "If you want to stay in this country you need to get used to it."

Then she huffs and tells me to hurry. "The post office branch you want is Great Portland Street," she says. "It opens at nine so we need to get going."

I pick up a piece of toast and move to the front door. "Are you sure you don't mind coming too?" I ask.

She scowls a little. "I've said I would, so I will," she says. "But if you try anything, you should know I can look after myself."

I shake my head. "If you don't trust me, just say. I'll happily go on my own."

She stares at me. "I don't trust you," she says. "And I don't want you making Mum's life any more dangerous than it already is. Things have been going wrong on her operation and for all I know it could be your fault. I'll get you to your post office," she adds. "And after today you stay away from her. You can go and be someone else's problem."

We get on a train and head towards London, sitting silently in a busy carriage that crawls along for about an hour through the huge city. Then we get the Underground, crushed into carriages like bait in a box. I hate it but I don't say anything and we surface somewhere called Oxford Circus, into another huge swarm of people. Petrol fumes clog the skies. The sun glares off the massive glass shopfronts. Cars inch forward down a wide street. I try and work out where I am but the city is too big and I have no idea. I have never been anywhere so big or so busy but Hayley slides through the crowds like the place was made for her. When I lag behind she turns back to me with her hands on her hips, then sets off again before I catch up. She steps out into the street, ignoring the traffic, weaving through the cars to the other side, then leads us down another road that is less busy and then finally to a crossroads where the grey, four-storey post office building is on our right.

And when I realise that this is the place, I feel urgency wash through me. I run round the outside of the building, desperate to find Dad, but I can't see him. I check the time, then the street name but they are both right. Fear and dread claw at me and I check my phone one more time but there are no messages. I spin round, staring at the crowds to check again, jumping to see over the mass of people but he is not here. He has not made it. I am on my own.

Hayley senses it. "You OK?" she asks.

"I thought he would be here. It is where we said we would meet."

"You heard what Mum said," she says. "They picked everyone up on the beach. He was never going to get here."

I almost force my muscles to contract, to hold myself upright and keep going. I don't know what to say so I don't say anything.

"Now what?"

"I'm going to get the parcel."

Hayley frowns. "It's not addressed to you," she says. "It's probably illegal to collect someone else's post."

But how can I let that stop me? I have faced soldiers and border guards. I have clung to the air as the waves pitched and the blackness called my name. I have survived and will continue to survive until I get the documents and find my dad. I tell her I don't care what she does, but I'm going to get the parcel.

Then I turn and head into the building.

Inside is a scruffy-looking retail area with rows of stationery and office supplies before an automated queuing system leads to three manned desks. When we reach the front I smile at the middle-aged assistant but I get nothing back.

"I'm here to collect a parcel," I say, and I push the piece of paper with my dad's name across the counter.

She grunts as if it is too much effort, then gets up heavily and goes out to a different room at the back. After what seems like years, she reappears carrying a very large brown envelope that appears to be stuffed with papers.

I get a brief sense of relief that the documents are actually here, before the tension rises again. She asks for ID and I pull my passport from my pocket then try to keep my hands still as I push it across the counter. She checks the passport then looks up sharply. "These names are different," she says. "I can only give it to someone with ID the same as the name on the envelope."

I stare at her, trying not to let my nerves show. "Can I see?" I ask, and when she shows me, I force a smile. "That's the way they do it in my country," I say. "We call each other by our second names but on formal documents they are the other way around. My dad's name is Sviatoslav Aleksander. Mine is Aleksander Sviatoslav. But you can see the surname is the same."

The woman checks and of course it is. She thinks about making a fuss but her eyes dart to the queue behind me and she decides not to. She tells me to sign a piece of paper and the envelope is mine. Within another minute I am outside with my heart still thumping.

And then a hand grabs my shoulder.

I stare up at the soft blond moustache and shaved head of Captain Ivanov and lurch away as I recognise him as one of the soldiers who came to arrest Dad, but his grip is too tight for me to break free.

I struggle with him but he pushes me into a wall and stops me from moving. And I can feel the gun in his jacket pocket push into my hip.

"Keep still," he says to me quietly, in my own language. "Or I will kill you in the street." He reaches down and takes the envelope from my hand. "I will take this, I think," he whispers. "We will go somewhere quiet and check what it is and if I am satisfied I will let you go. Otherwise I will shoot you."

I twist in his grip, but he digs the gun hard into me and I can see in his eyes that he is prepared to shoot so I stop. "What have you done with my dad?" I hiss.

He looks surprised. "Weren't you at the boat?" he says, before waving the envelope at me. "It doesn't matter. This envelope is what really matters."

About a hundred metres away is a grassy park with a statue of a man on horseback in the middle. He pushes me roughly along the busy streets but nobody seems to notice.

We cross the road towards the park where there is more space. As we turn a corner towards the entrance, I prepare to run. I tense and am about to spring forward when Hayley appears in front of us out of nowhere and appears to trip, bundling into Ivanov and knocking him away from her. He stumbles forward, shoving me hard into the iron railing as he flails out to stop his fall, but he doesn't let go. Hayley's eyes widen when she sees her plan didn't work, then she keeps walking into the crowd, with her hand in the air as a fake apology. The soldier reaches out and refixes his grip on my collar.

"Stupid Londoners," he barks. "So clumsy. Let's just get this done."

There is no way to stop Hayley without giving her away, so I keep walking, crossing the road to the park. And when she appears in front of us and appears to trip I use it, pushing him more off balance as he stumbles into the railings. His hands rise to protect himself and I tear myself free. I rip the envelope from the soldier's fingers and take off as fast as I can.

I run, through the heaving streets, through the swarm of people, down a road busy with shops and restaurants, twisting to look over my shoulder to see he is right behind me. I duck into a road on the right and then turn again, but I can't shake him off. We burst into a wide street with old buildings on either side and I tear up the pavement, then dart across to the other side but as I turn to look I think he may be getting closer. There is less traffic and I can hear the slap of his shoes on the ground, then he shouts at me.

"Stop or I will shoot you in the street."

People stare, but they don't understand the language and I don't stop. Pain burns in my muscles, but anger drives me on. An alleyway opens up on my left and I lurch into it before he has rounded the corner behind me, then sprint down through the waste bins and air-conditioning units until I reach the end. But I've made a mistake. All that's in front of me is a solid brick wall with no way through or round. I am trapped.

I flatten myself against a wall and try and hide behind a large metal waste bin, watching as the soldier rounds the corner and runs past the alley. His footsteps pound on the pavement and I hear the rush of his breathing and then he is gone. I close my eyes and breathe out, then pant as my body tries to recover. I slump back against the wall of the alley then allow myself to sink down until I am sitting on the ground.

Just as his blue eyes appear round the corner once again. And this time I have nowhere to run.

He moves slowly towards me, then checks over his shoulder, but there is no one around. He takes the gun out of his pocket and points it at me so I get up with raised hands, then stand there staring at him. I still have the envelope in my hand and he tells me to put it on the ground then back away until I reach the wall, but I refuse. I don't know what's in it, but this is why we have run. This is why we crossed those borders and took those risks. This is what my dad risked his life for. I am not going to just hand it over, whatever he threatens. I keep hold of it as I back off, until I feel the hard brick behind me. I glance around the alley but there is no way I can think of to protect it.

He scowls at me, his blue eyes narrowing in anger.

"Put the envelope down," he hisses. "If you want to live, you will give it to me."

"Go to hell," I say in English.

He smiles, a thin nasty smile. "Very well," he says. "This seems like as good a place as any. I will kill you and take it. Is that what you want?"

"Will you leave my dad alone if I give it to you?" I say.

The question surprises him. "Yes," he says quickly, but I can tell from his expression and the speed of his reply that he is lying.

I shake my head. "You've taken my home and my family," I say. "You may as well take me."

I drop the envelope on the ground to my side then

stand with my back to the wall and my hands in front of my chest.

There is nowhere to go. I stand facing him, staring at the cruelty in his eyes. He stands with his back to the alleyway entrance, hiding the gun and me from anyone who might look down. I brace myself for the pain, then focus on his fingers as he raises the weapon. I see his fingers rest on the trigger.

Then I spring forward and to the side. He hesitates for a moment before the explosion fills the air. I am already moving and I can't change direction. Pain rips through my chest...

I stand with my back to the wall. He stands with his back to the alleyway entrance. I brace myself for the pain, then focus on his fingers as he raises the weapon. I see his fingers rest on the trigger. I spring forward then hesitate for the shortest moment, before twisting down and to the side. The explosion fills the air and I am already moving and can't change direction. I feel a sharp sting in my shoulder as the bullet skims my skin then thumps into the wall, but I don't stop moving, charging into him with all my might, forcing him back into the metal bin, slamming his arm hard into the steel to try and make him drop the gun. We crash to the ground but he doesn't let go of it. He claws at me with his other hand, raking my face, but I ignore it and focus on keeping the gun away from me, using the momentum to push him hard into the wall. He grunts, but the shock of my attack is wearing off and he is a trained soldier. Slowly he forces his arm round until he takes control again. He rolls over, on top of me and now all I can do is struggle against him as he brings the gun over me. He glares at me and there is murder in his eyes. He is about to pull the trigger.

I do the only thing I can and give in. For a moment. As his finger pulls back, I give way and now the gun swings over my chest and past it. My hands close over his and I wrench his wrist and twist it just as he fires. The explosion rings out and the bullet screams past my side and into his knee.

Shock bursts into his eyes. He gasps and rears back in pain. I shove him off me and spring to my feet, kicking the gun from his hand so it clatters under the bin, then turn to face him, but the fight has gone out of him. His knee is a mess and there is a lot of blood on the ground. He stares at me, but I don't want to look at him and now I can hear sirens. People have heard the gunshots, and faces stare into the alleyway. I can't afford to be here when the police arrive so I dash to pick up the envelope then sprint out of the alley, pushing aside the few onlookers. As I run up the street, two police cars blare past me towards the alley. I turn, briefly, to see some of the crowd pointing at me, then I turn a corner and hurry away. Within moments I am back on the busy street and lost in a sea of people.

15

BEFORE

Dad puts his phone down on the picnic table in front of us and drags his fingers across the screen to enlarge the coastline from Amsterdam to Calais. We have filled the car up with petrol for the second time, but Dad says he wants to let the engine cool down because it's been getting hotter as the hours have gone past. When I asked him if he thought it was OK, he snapped at me that of course it was, then opened the bonnet and stared at it as if willing it to make the last few hundred kilometres. It just needs to last another half a day, we are both thinking. Just a few more hours.

Dad mutters the names of the ports out loud but I am pretty sure he is talking to himself, not to me. He has hardly spoken to me all morning and when I have tried to talk to him, he has told me he was concentrating. He hasn't mentioned my gift or Mum and he hasn't even tried calling Grandmother, although I did when we stopped before. She didn't answer. I wonder if he has given up.

"Ostend or Calais," he says twice, before shaking his head and looking up at the sign by the side of the car park, which tells us it is 231 kilometres to Antwerp, 268 to Brussels and 570 to Paris. I look at the map and I can see Ostend is closer, but he has said there is much more traffic through Calais.

Eventually he checks his watch and stands up to go. "Calais," he says. "Even if they are there looking for us, there are more people to hide among. We go to Calais. And then we find a way across."

16

AFTER

I call Hayley to say I'm OK and thanks for helping, but she just seems angrier with me than ever. She accuses me of being watched, like I wanted the soldier to find me, and says I was lucky her mum told her to look after me because she wouldn't have done it otherwise. Then she tells me she's going to go back home on a train at four o'clock and if I want to go too I should meet her at Victoria Station. I don't want to upset her more so I say I will, then I sit in a park for hours with the envelope clutched tight to my chest. I don't know what's in it but I know it's bad so I don't want to open it in public. And I can't remember what happened on the boat after the shooting started. I need to talk to Rachel and find out what information her friend has got. Then I'll get out of their lives forever.

Hayley turns up about five minutes before the train is due to leave and sits silent and stern-faced, messaging on her phone for most of the way. We sit across from each other in a bank of four seats, and when we are alone I try and thank her again but she just spits something at me about danger and bringing violence into their lives. Then a big guy sits down in one of the spare seats and spends the rest of the journey playing solitaire on his laptop. We sit in silence.

As soon as we get into the house, it seems to pour out. Hayley tells Rachel what happened then she announces that she thinks I should go. Rachel's face sets and she tells Hayley to stop being so rude. They both go into the kitchen and for a minute I don't hear what they are saying until suddenly the shouting starts. Hayley yells that all I'm doing is putting them in danger and how many border force agents need to die before Rachel realises, but Rachel laughs and asks if Hayley thought about danger when she charged at an armed man. Hayley says it was my fault for putting her in that position and now she's had enough. She screams that the job is the only thing Rachel cares about and tells her to think about what would happen if Rachel was hurt. Rachel yells back, something about doing the right thing and now I can hear the tears in both their voices. I need to leave. I will find somewhere else to go. Now I've got the envelope I can take it to someone and help my dad. I just need to check what's in it first.

I ignore the shouting and tip the envelope out on to the table in front of me, filling the afternoon with war. Maps of troop movements; orders to take up offensive positions; times, dates and locations of strategic attacks. Lightning strikes; no prisoners to be taken; lists, numbers and destruction. Detailed instructions on suppression of the media. Infiltration techniques; propaganda messages. Moving in the new; moving out the old.

And then there are the photographs. Rushed photocopies mostly, but clear enough and chilling. The destruction of villages; the aftermath of bombardments. Temporary encampments with barbed wire and scared faces. Trials, executions and graves. Anything my dad thought could wake the world up is spread on the table in front of me. And I finally understand how brave he must have been.

The house is quiet. The shouting has stopped and I realise that Rachel and Hayley are standing behind me, staring over my shoulder at the documents on the table. I don't know how long they've been there, but there is a shocked silence in the room and a look of fear on both their faces. Rachel leans forward and picks up a photograph.

"Did you see any of this?" she asks.

I shake my head. "Stories came down from the

mountains, but it was hidden. We noticed the new people and the changes in rules. I didn't know about the detail, but I guess Dad must have."

Hayley sits down heavily and turns a picture towards her. Rachel starts to say something, then stops herself. Hayley asks me what some of the words mean and I tell her. She stares at me for a moment, then looks away. Then I remember.

"I'd better be going," I say. "And leave you two alone."

And I think it's what she wants, but she just stares at me. Her eyes glance back to the photograph she is holding until she pushes it away into the rest of the pile.

"I'm so sorry," says Hayley quietly. "I had no idea."

I look from her to Rachel, who nods to me. "Don't go yet," she says gently. "I'm worried about your dad. My friend said the border force didn't pick him up and no one else got through." She frowns. "And if he wasn't at the post office..."

A horrible fear runs through me like ice. "It was chaotic at the beach," I say. "I thought he got on the boat, but maybe he didn't."

Rachel frowns. "I'll get a colleague to put out an alert and we'll get the French to look for him too." She sighs. "Try and stay strong," she adds. "And you can stay here as long as you need."

I glance at Hayley. "Are you sure?" I ask.

Hayley's eyes flick towards the pictures again. "It doesn't seem real," she says. "I'm sorry," she says again. "You shouldn't go."

"Besides," Rachel adds, "you've still got the kitchen to paint."

She is trying to break the tension but I don't know what to say. For a moment the silence is deafening. Rachel seems to sense it and she looks at her watch. "I'm starving," she says. "Why don't we eat?"

They order a curry, choosing something red and spicy for me, then we sit at the table awkwardly. Rachel and Hayley try hard to talk but it is stumbling and difficult, until Hayley suddenly blurts out that the photos look like pictures from a history book and she didn't think things like that would happen now. Her hand whips up to her red face and she stares at me in shock, but I don't mind as I would rather talk than sit in silence. She asks me a question and I notice Rachel tense, unsure of how I will react, but it feels like such a relief that people will listen and believe me that I just want to tell them what I can. Hayley asks another question about opposition and fighting then asks almost incredulously why we didn't see it coming. But I don't know the answer and now she looks embarrassed.

I try to explain and they listen as the time goes by. We sit while the food goes cold and all the little things I never realised I knew just pour out. I tell them about the curfew and how the programmes on the TV changed. I tell them about the trucks that moved around at night and how I would watch for faces on the way to school and write their names in a book when one was missing. Then Hayley asks me more about school and I tell them some of the things that happened, more clearly now because these are the things I know. I tell them about how the textbooks changed and how there were never enough, and about which teachers were fair and which were not. When I mention the guy who taught me maths, Hayley says she never knew how lucky she was and Rachel makes one of her stupid jokes about being surprised Hayley has ever met her maths teacher, given her last set of marks. Hayley pulls a face and rolls her eyes so dramatically that I can't help smiling. My eyes meet Hayley's and she splutters into a laugh and somehow the mood changes. She tells a story about her school. "It's nothing like yours," she starts, "and it's just a silly story..." But it makes me laugh. And for a moment we are all laughing at some kid who tried to cheat but learned the wrong answers and who will never know how much difference he has made.

The subject changes and Rachel talks a little about being a police officer, until Hayley interrupts to complain about what it's like to be a police officer's daughter. Jokes, adventures and exaggerations. Kids at school, dumb criminals and ruined cop shows on TV. And for the shortest moment I feel normal again. In a home, feeling full, talking nonsense with friends. Until I look down and notice my hand is shaking. I drop the spoon then reach to pick it up and knock over a glass. I try and reach down again, but now I can't seem to move my fingers and I don't know how I am supposed to stand up. Hayley is on her feet, rushing to the kitchen to get a cloth, but Rachel comes towards me. She takes the spoon from my fingers and puts it down, then wraps her arms round me and hugs me hard.

"It's going to be OK," she whispers. "It's going to be OK."

17

BEFORE

"Keep your eyes open," Dad says. "This might be the sort of place we can find someone to help."

We are sitting at an outside table of a fast-food restaurant at a service station about twelve kilometres before we reach Dunkirk. Time seems to be drifting by but we just wait. Dad is tense and irritable, snapping at me not to make a mess when I start picking apart the paper cup I've been drinking from. He still hasn't said anything more about Mum and I don't want to ask while he's in this mood. I slurp again at the last of the drink, then tell him I'm going to the bathroom.

There are facilities inside, but there is also a sign to an old shower block round the back where there are fewer people, so I go there. But as soon as I walk in I wonder if I've made a mistake.

The room is full of people talking in a language I don't understand, until silence seems to crash down as soon as I go in. Scared faces look up at me, large eyes full of fear. An older man barks something at a boy who is near the door and I see his eyes dart to the lock, which he must have forgotten to use. I raise my hands.

"It's OK," I say in English. "No problem. It's OK."

There are about twenty of them. Dark-haired and dark-eyed, squashed into the small room. On the side, a man with only one arm is struggling to unwrap a chocolate bar. A young woman has burn marks on her face and hands. In a corner near an old sink, a mother is washing her child's face and the running water is now the only sound. The little girl stares at me, then looks away bashfully as I catch her eye.

"Syria?" I ask.

A man nods. He tries a smile and I smile back.

"Going to England?"

More nods now.

"Me too," I say. "We're going to England."

A young man scowls. "Easy for you," he says. "Buy ticket, go to England."

But I shake my head. "Same as you," I say.

He laughs. "Easy for white boy," he says, but then one of the old men snaps something at him and he stops.

I look around and nod to them. "Good luck," I say. Then I back out of the room and they lock the door behind me.

When I tell Dad he looks up sharply, then twists to stare around the service area. Behind the restaurant and the shower block is the main lorry park and he tells me to move so that we are sitting at the end table where we can see.

"They're here for a reason," he says. "Maybe it's what we need."

Almost immediately, a silver Mercedes convertible rips into the lorry park and swerves into one of the lorry spaces. Two men get out. One is European-looking, dressed in smart clothes with his phone clamped between his shoulder and his ear, barking instructions at someone. The other is younger and looks African. The older man points back towards the entrance to the services and watches as the younger man jogs off in that direction. Then he looks at the chunky Rolex on his wrist and hurries to the shower block, thumping on the door and going inside when it opens. Two minutes later, he comes out on his own, the phone still against his ear. He stands next to his car and stares back at the entrace until a large Dernbach Logistics lorry carrying chilled goods turns in. The man waves to it and puts the phone in his pocket, then waits for the lorry to park and the driver to get out. They speak briefly as the driver hurries to the back and opens the chilled container. Then the man goes back to the shower block and comes back half walking, half jogging, leading the Syrians to the lorry.

Suddenly Dad is on his feet. "We need to speak to him," he says. "Wait here."

He steps out and strides towards the lorry. Rolex guy ignores him until it is obvious he is going towards them then suddenly he turns and grabs Dad, pulling him to the side of the lorry out of sight. At the same time, the driver slams shut the door of the lorry just as the first Syrians arrive. They protest but he just yells at them to get back to the shower block. Then he hurries back round to where Dad is. There is anger on his face and he reaches into his jacket for something. I need to know what's happening and I don't have another way of finding out.

I run forward, pushing my way through the Syrians until I reach Dad. The European has him up against the side of the lorry.

"England, England," Dad is saying, but the man doesn't understand him. He shoves him hard against the passenger door and pulls a knife out of his jacket pocket.

"Who are you? Where are you from?" he says in

*French, but Dad doesn't speak French and he doesn't
know how to answer.*

*"Here," I say, holding out my passport. And then my
time is gone.*

I have no choice but to let it play.

"Here," I say, holding out my passport. "*Vous pouvez
voir d'où nous venons.*" You can see where we're from.

The man sees me and holds the knife closer to Dad.
I don't know what else to do except show him my
passport. He looks at it and I see his eyes narrow.

He waves at the lorry. "You not police?" he says in
stuttering English.

"No. We're not police."

"You want to go to England. Like this?"

Dad nods. "Yes," he says. "England."

The guy thinks for a moment then says something
to the driver in French, too fast for me to understand
properly. Then he tells us to wait. The driver goes back
round to open the lorry again while the first man goes
to get the Syrians back. We watch as they hurry over,
running now to the open container, moving boxes
aside to clamber into the chilled space. The first man
gets in then turns in shock but the others are already
climbing up behind him and they force him down

towards the back.

"We go too?" Dad says, but Rolex guy shakes his head.

"Need to pay first."

"I can pay now," Dad says.

"No. You don't pay me. Another in a week," he says.

Dad argues. "That's too late. We need to go today."

Then Rolex guy's phone rings. As he answers it I see him tense, then turn to the driver and spit the word "police". He runs to the back of the lorry with his phone still clamped to his ear, urging the Syrians to move faster. But there is a problem.

From inside the lorry I can hear their voices rise in distress. The man ignores them, his eyes fixed on the entrance to the services, his phone hard against his ear. Dad is trying to talk to the driver, but I am staring at the Syrians. Their breath steams in front of them as soon as they climb up and they immediately wrap their arms round their thinly covered bodies. The ones further back are shivering and they complain, but it is in a language the man doesn't understand. He just pushes at them to climb up and now there are only three left to get on.

"Police, police, police," he repeats, running round to

close the door to the lorry before the last one is even on. He starts to close it but I know there is something very wrong about this.

"Wait," I shout at him. "*Attendez!*" I scream, but he ignores me. And I need to know what is going on.

I push in front of the last Syrian and climb up on to the back of the lorry. Almost immediately the door slams behind me and we are plunged into darkness. Someone switches on the torch of a phone for a moment and the light throws shadows all around. Figures huddle together in the back of the lorry, pulling themselves together behind the boxes there. But the only thing I can think about is the intense cold that hits me. I have heard that smugglers use refrigerated lorries to avoid detection by dogs, but this is crazy. If these people spend any length of time in this freezing lorry they will be in big trouble and they already know it. But they are desperate. They argue in whispers for a few seconds then go quiet, ignoring the cold and huddling together to try and keep warm. They beckon me to join them, to offer me some of their warmth and I feel hands rubbing my arms as the group welcomes me in. We feel the engine roar into life and the lorry starts to reverse.

And I am out of time.

I watch as Rolex guy slams the door behind the last Syrian then runs round to where the driver is sitting in the cab. I follow him and grab at his shoulder, spinning him round. "It's too cold," I shout. "*Trop froid. Trop froid.*"

He pushes me away roughly, so that I hit the lorry hard, but I don't give up. I grab his shirt with both hands and shout at him. "You want me to make a fuss?" I scream. "You want me to tell the police about this lorry? *Trop froid,*" I shout. "You need to make it warmer."

The driver starts the engine and stares at us out of his window. The younger guy that was sent to watch for the police is running down the road towards us. Rolex guy reaches into his jacket to where his knife is but I don't care about that and just yell at him again. "It's too cold," I shout in French. "They will die!" And at last I see something change in his expression.

Rolex guy turns to the driver and barks something at him and now I see the shock in his eyes too. The driver leans across to some controls and pushes a button and immediately the electric hum from the back of the lorry stops. The driver looks past Rolex guy at me.

"OK, OK," he says. "OK now."

Rolex guy says something to him and the man nods. "Not cold now," he says. "Much better."

"*Allez*," Rolex guy snaps, and the driver pulls the lorry out and away. Rolex guy stares back into the service station for a moment, but there is no sign of the police and he seems to relax.

Dad turns to him. "Can you help us?" he says. "*Aidez nous?*"

The younger man runs up and gets back into their car. Rolex guy turns to Dad and stares at him.

"Next week," he says. "Another lorry."

But Dad shakes his head. "It needs to be today. Do you know someone?"

The guy hesitates, catching my eye for a moment before checking his watch again and leading us quickly to his car. As he opens the driver's door he takes a piece of paper out of the car and scribbles a phone number on it. "There is a boat in Calais," he says. "A team from England. Go to Calais and call this number. Ask for Ronnie."

Then he revs the engine and goes. The whole meeting took less than three minutes.

18

AFTER

My phone wakes me, sawing through the silence, insistent and urgent. I lurch up and stare around me. Light steals in through closed shutters. The house is silent except for the buzzing, which won't stop. But there is only one person it can be. I answer it.

"Yeah?"

Ronnie's voice burns down the line. I can almost hear him chewing his nails. "Where are you?"

I stand up with the duvet still round my shoulders and move to the window. "In the town. I found a hostel where they didn't ask questions."

"We're going again," he says. "I want you there. I'll pick you up outside the Prince George pub on Trafalgar Street. Look it up and I'll see you there in fifteen."

"No," I say. "I don't want to be involved."

"Got a better job, did you?"

I don't answer him. "I don't want to be involved," I say again. But he cuts the call before I've finished the words.

Hayley must hear me because she appears at the door, dressed in jeans and a dark hoodie. She seems nervous and leans on the doorframe with her arms crossed.

"You OK?" she says to me.

"Where's your mum?"

She comes in and walks through to the kitchen. "She's gone out. She had to go to some meeting."

"I've just been invited to the same one."

Her eyes widen. "You're still involved?"

I shake my head. "No," I say. "But I think I know where they're meeting Stripes. Is it OK to call her?"

But Hayley shakes her head. "You can't call her when she's undercover. No calls, ever," she says. "We just sit here and wait, hoping she'll be back safe. That's the deal."

"But somebody needs to be there and see who this guy is. Get his number plate or something. That's what she said the other night."

"There's a number we can call. Someone above her. We can tell them."

But I shake my head. "I don't think we should speak to anyone else," I say. "They will want to know who I am. They will want to know why I'm staying here."

Hayley has opened the dishwasher and started unloading it. When I speak she looks up sharply. "You mean Mum might get into trouble?"

"I don't know but I don't want to risk anything. We can't tell anyone else without checking with her."

I help her put some things away then go back to the lounge.

"I guess we wait until next time then," I say.

Her face appears at the doorway. "How long do you think that will be?"

"I don't know. I don't think they're very regular."

Hayley looks nervous. "When we spoke about Mum going undercover," she says, "I didn't think it would be like this. But things started going wrong a while ago and all I do is sit at home worrying about her. I know she's doing the right thing but..." She tails off. Then she looks at me. "Are these people as dangerous as the ones in London?"

I don't know what to say. She looks nervous, but I don't want to lie.

"They're not soldiers, but..." I shrug helplessly.

She nods. "OK," she says. "We'll do it. You know what he looks like. And we just need to see what car he gets into?"

I hesitate. "I don't know if we should—" I start, but she cuts me off.

"If you're scared they'll recognise you, don't come,"

she says. "But tell me where they're meeting and I'll go."

I hesitate again, but she just glares at me. Her hands are planted firmly on her hips and her chin juts out in determination. "If it makes my mum any safer you owe us that at least."

Eventually I nod. "Fine," I say. "But we shouldn't take any risks. It's a busy part of town. We'll just watch until he gets back to his car and get the number. Then come home where it's safe."

She nods. "Fine," she repeats.

I tell her about the pub on Trafalgar Street and she finds it on a map and we get ready to leave. As we leave the house I turn to her. "Your mother is helping me," I say. "I don't want to do the wrong thing."

And now she smiles. "Adults never ask for help until it's too late," she says. "So if we don't tell her until it's too late, she can't get too mad, can she?"

I look ahead before we turn the corner into Trafalgar Street but Stripes isn't there yet. Hayley has found me an old baseball cap and a pair of large sunglasses that make some sort of disguise and we wait on the opposite side of the road to the pub. After a few minutes I see the bulk of the BMW stuttering through the traffic. It halts at a pedestrian crossing, and then Stripes is there too. He drops the same black rucksack into the open door, then disappears back into the crowd, melting away before I really get a chance to see him go. I turn to Hayley but she is already moving. So I pull the cap down over my eyes and follow her.

We don't go far. Stripes chooses one of the roads busiest with people then stops at a coffee shop, sitting outside and sipping on an espresso. We keep going, then stop at a milkshake bar about fifty metres further on. We order vanilla shakes and watch, but it doesn't look like he's going anywhere and I wonder if it's going to be a wasted trip, until I realise he must be waiting to get the money and the bag on the way back. A waitress puts our shakes down in front of us and we do our best to look casual.

"Tell me about the things that have been going wrong," I say.

Hayley sips at her drink, glancing towards Stripes as if to check he can't hear her answer. He is facing away from us, tapping on his phone. "She was put on the job because the smugglers had too many details of the border force operations so they decided to use a police officer. The last time a patrol tried to stop a boat the smugglers were ready for them. There was a fight and an officer drowned."

And now I know why she is so worried. "You think there's someone from the border force talking to the smugglers? Putting your mum in danger?"

Hayley scowls and I see the muscles in her arms and neck tense. She looks ready to take on the world and suddenly I feel a desperate need to reassure her. But I can't. "Mum hates what the smugglers are doing," she says. "But these people make so much money they'll never stop." She breaks off and laughs. "You know this better than me, right?" she says.

"I am glad there are people in this country who care," I say, but before I can say anything else, Hayley's eyes have moved past me to focus on Stripes again. "He's moving," she says. "Time to go."

We wait outside the pub and watch the routine repeat itself. Stripes leans into the car and comes away with the bag then hurries away.

"He must be going to his car now," Hayley whispers, and I nod.

"He's in more of a hurry too," I say. "Probably because he's got a gun in that bag."

Hayley's eyes widen, but her face is determined and she keeps her vision locked on Stripes. We squeeze through the crowd, keeping about thirty metres behind him, but he never turns round. At the end of the lane he heads left, up past the train station then further up a hill until we come to a road of white houses. He walks halfway down it until he reaches one with scaffolding around the front and a huge blue plastic sheet across the roof. There is a yellow builder's skip on the drive that is full of rubble and the whole house seems deserted. Suddenly he slows and turns, staring at us, then past us before looking around him. We can't stop so we get closer, but he doesn't seem interested in a couple of kids. He takes his phone out of his pocket and I slow down as we go past, bending to tie my shoelace as he speaks.

"Yeah," he says. "I'll be here for an hour. Come and pick it up."

I stand and we keep going, passing him slowly, then crossing the road so we keep moving but can still see him. Hayley pushes playfully at my shoulder and laughs innocently, but I can see her looking past me across at him. She keeps up the act until suddenly she stops and her face turns serious.

"He's gone round the back," she says. "Now what do we do?"

"We go back and tell your mum," I say. "Then she can get this place watched."

But Hayley shakes her head. "He doesn't live here," she hisses. "Look at it. The place hasn't got a roof. It's just a place for a meeting."

I stare at it and she's right. There is no sign of life anywhere in the house; the curtains are all open but I can't see any furniture. "And we can't just stand here," she adds. "We need to hide."

It feels like we're getting sucked into something we should avoid, but there isn't time to think. I grab her wrist and we cross the road again, fast, ducking into the driveway on the other side of the house that Stripes went into. There is a gate on the side, but it is open, leading to a garden that is also full of building materials.

I peer round the edge of the building, but Stripes must have gone inside.

I turn back to Hayley, but she isn't there.

A noise above startles me and I twist to look, in time to see Hayley swing herself gracefully over a scaffolding pole before landing lightly on the boards

170

above. She leans down and reaches out to take my wrist and I am surprised at the strength she has to pull me up. I am panting with exertion but she just smiles at me.

"County champion gymnast," she whispers. "You need to get fitter."

I hold my finger to my lips but she has already moved, crawling along the boards until she reaches a window. She glances in then drops down urgently as someone moves inside. We wait for thirty seconds then crawl past until we reach a ladder that goes up further, climbing it silently until we are level with the huge blue plastic sheet spread across the roof. Hayley lifts the edge. Inside, the half-constructed roof space glows bluc as light spills in through unglazed windows, casting shadows across the building materials and tools that litter the floor. She pulls it back further then slides into the gap before lowering herself silently inside. I follow, and she winces as I land more heavily, but nobody comes. We creep to the side of the space where a large hole opens out to the landing below then lie still, listening.

There is no ladder and no easy way down without being trapped so we lie with our heads near the edge. Stripes is moving about, his footsteps echoing through the house as dust floats in the air and our breathing measures time for minutes. When there is a bang on the door it rings out like a shot.

The front door opens then shuts. We hear footsteps on the bare floors then voices moving inside the house.

"Did you count it?"

"It's all there."

"Any problems?"

"No."

The new voice is deep and English. Stripes's voice seems thin in comparison. And needy, somehow.

"And Ronnie's behaving himself?"

"Yeah."

There is a pause while we lie there. The new man seems to be thinking. Eventually he speaks again.

"OK," he says. "I think it's time we got rid of the policewoman."

My insides go cold.

"What do you want to do?"

"Get round to her house and pick her up. Take her to the boathouse and find out what she knows."

"And then?"

"Next trip across, she doesn't come back."

He says it bluntly and Hayley gasps next to me. She sits upright quickly, knocking a piece of wood from where it was balancing. As it falls heavily to the ground with a thud, the voices below suddenly cut off. Then we hear running up the stairs.

We jump to our feet silently, but it is too late. Below we can hear the two men at the top of the stairs. We shrink back from the edge, but I can almost feel their eyes staring up through the open hole into the roof space.

"Who's up there?" the new man shouts.

We don't answer. Hayley looks at me then flicks her wide eyes over towards the gap where we got in. Her face has drained of colour and I can see her hands shaking slightly. And I don't need my gift to know they're coming so I just nod and we start to move as quietly as we can.

"Who's up there?" the man shouts again, then he tells Stripes to pass him a ladder. We move quickly but so does he. Hayley is at the gap in the plastic sheet, but it is much harder to climb up than it was to scramble down. She drags across a work bench as the top of the ladder appears through the hole. I run over and try and kick it back down, but it is too far through the gap and I can't lever it away. The man is halfway up and grabs at my ankle but misses. He is clean shaven and handsome with short grey hair and bright-blue eyes, but there is a cruelty in them that shocks me. I kick down at him again, catching him on the shoulder and he cries out.

And now I see the gun.

Glass churns in my stomach. I have slowed him down for a moment but we have seen each other and I have seen the ruthlessness in his eyes. He yells at Stripes to get outside and stop us getting out, then starts climbing the ladder again. Hayley has scrambled up and out on to the scaffolding. She yells at me to get out and I run to her as the man reaches the top of the ladder. I half jump on to the workbench and throw myself up towards Hayley's outstretched arm. She reaches out and latches on to my shirt, pulling me forward towards the gap in the plastic and I squeeze through on to the planks of the scaffolding outside. Just as the man steps off the top of the ladder.

And Stripes appears in the garden.

"Run," Hayley screams, leading the way along the scaffolding, ducking under a metal bar then scrambling down a ladder to the level below. She keeps going, towards the side of the house, then skids to a stop as Stripes races round the corner to stare up at us. I can't see a gun, but he is a big man and we are trapped on the scaffolding outside the first floor of the house. The other man has gone back down inside and Hayley stops suddenly as he appears at one of the windows. She turns and pushes me away and we run back across the front of the house to the other side. Stripes runs across the garden and the man inside runs through the house. We are trapped on the scaffolding. There is nowhere to go.

"We need to jump," Hayley yells. She reaches the corner of the house and points to the neighbouring garden, which is separated from ours by a brick wall about five feet high and two metres away. "Land on the wall then roll into the next garden."

"Are you mad?" I ask, but she doesn't stop to listen.

"Do what I do," she says, and then she just takes off.

She climbs over the final scaffolding barrier and braces herself on the poles overhanging the driveway. Stripes stretches up from below but he can't quite reach. She jumps, with her feet together and arms outstretched, flying through the air like a bird for a moment, until she lands perfectly on the top of the wall, bending her knees calmly as she lands, then dropping down once more into the next-door garden.

She turns and stares at me. She is fine, but I don't know if I can do that. Behind me I hear a window open and I know it is only moments before the man catches me.

I step out on the metal poles and jump.

I slip as I jump, landing heavily on the ground at the side of the house. Something cracks in my ankle and my leg erupts in pain. Stripes looms over me.

I open my eyes and try again.

I jump, landing hard on the wall. My right foot lands on the edge of the bricks, then skids off so that my foot goes over, but most of my body slams hard into the wall. I tip backwards, reeling out of control with my arms over my head, falling back into the garden of the house. Stripes looms over me.

I open my eyes and turn to look behind me. The man is opening the window and climbing out on to the scaffolding now, and I realise I've been stupid. I shouldn't have turned to look. Because now there is no more time to practise.

19

BEFORE

We head back to the car but Dad doesn't start the engine straight away. He just sits still for a few minutes, thinking.

"Dad," I say. "We need to go."

He nods, but he still doesn't move. Eventually he swivels in his seat to face me.

"You used it again, didn't you?" he says.

I try to read in his expression whether he is angry or not, but I can't. I nod slowly. "I climbed on board the lorry to see what was wrong," I say. "If I'd done it in real time I would have been trapped on the lorry so it seemed like the only way. Otherwise I probably would have died with the others."

Dad puffs out his cheeks and leans back. "I guess you saved them," he says.

I grunt. "Still think it's a curse?" I ask.

Dad rubs his face with his hands and sighs. "I had the gift too," he says quietly. "Your grandmother started teaching me to use it when I was about eighteen and I thought it was the most amazing thing I had ever known. I practised and practised until I had five or six seconds. Grandmother said she thought I could get much more."

His words surprise me. Why hadn't he told me

before? How could he hate it so much if he'd had it himself? He stretches out to put his hands on the steering wheel and leans back in his seat.

"And then when I was eighteen I realised how terrible it could be. One day in winter a group of us decided to go fishing at the lake, except when we got there we found it was all frozen over. We were messing around and someone suggested running across the frozen water for a dare. None of us were stupid enough to try it because we all knew how dangerous going through the ice could be, except I thought I would be clever and see what would happen if I ran across."

Dad crosses his arms round himself and I can see the pain of the memory etched on his face. "I took the five seconds I had and ran across the lake. It was a miracle but I managed to get to the other side and the ice held. Then I decided to show off and I did it for real."

He breaks off. "So what was the problem?" I ask.

"The problem was that your mum's brother figured if it would hold me, it would hold him. He took it as a challenge and ran out after me. The ice cracked and he went in. We never got him out. And I never used my gift again. Eventually I stopped knowing how."

There is silence in the car.

"It wasn't your fault..." I start, but Dad's head whips round and he stares at me.

"Of course it was my fault," he says bitterly. "If I hadn't used the gift none of us would have tried anything so stupid. He would still be alive."

"But a million other things would be different too," I say. "I wouldn't be alive! If my uncle hadn't died you wouldn't have married Mum and I wouldn't have been born. Would that be better?" I ask.

A cloud of uncertainty fills Dad's eyes.

"And then maybe those Syrians would all die in that lorry, or maybe you wouldn't have got across the border," I add. "You can't think like that, Dad," I say firmly. "You can only do what you think is right."

Dad laughs without humour. "My son is teaching me right from wrong," he says, but I shake my head.

"You taught me right from wrong, remember?" I say. "And you taught me to do everything I can to help people who need it." I reach out and rest my arm on his. "That includes using my gift," I say. "I just need you to trust me."

Dad sighs and places his hand over mine. "I..." he starts, but he can't seem to find the words. "It's hard," he says, "because I never even trusted myself."

"Please try, Dad?" I urge. "And I promise I will tell you if I'm going to use the gift."

He nods quickly then he starts the engine. "I arranged to meet this guy Ronnie in Calais," he says. "I just hope he comes through for us." He turns to me and smiles for the first time since we left home.

"I'm glad you're with me," he says. "I'm sorry I've been so hard."

I smile back. "That's OK," I say.

"I'm just so worried about getting it wrong," he says. "Life is just one leap into the darkness after another." He puts the car in gear and pulls out. "Maybe a few seconds is all we need to know where we're going to land."

20

AFTER

I jump. Landing hard on the wall. My right foot lands on the edge of the bricks, but I drop down fast on to my haunches, so my momentum slows. My foot goes over the edge but I tip forward, reeling out of control with my arms over my head, falling forward into the garden of the next-door house. Hayley reaches out and grabs my shoulders, protecting my head as I drop and breaking my fall.

"Graceful as a brick," she whispers, but there is no time to respond. She hauls me up and we run across the garden, past a climbing frame to a set of wooden furniture at the back fence. Stripes stares at us over it, but it is not easy to climb on his own. I turn and see the other man who is watching from the scaffolding, but he is in the open now and there is no sign of the gun. We drag a wooden seat to the fence then climb up and over and race down the side of the house and out into the street, running until we reach a bus stop where a bus is about to pull out. We jump on and clamber up the stairs and sit at the back. As the bus pulls away I see Stripes and the other man staring around the street looking for us, but they don't look up.

And eventually we are out of sight.

We huddle on the back seat, away from the other passengers.

"They're going to kill my mum."

When she speaks, a wave of guilt washes through me although I don't know why. Hayley is trying not to cry. There is terror in her eyes.

"Call her," I insist.

She hesitates, then takes out her phone and dials a number. I can hear the sound of ringing but no one answers. As she takes it away from her ear a text buzzes.

CAN'T TALK RIGHT NOW

"Damn!" she says. "We're going in the wrong direction. We need to get off the bus now."

She slams her thumb into the red button and rings the bell frantically, then runs to the front of the bus and down the stairs. Within moments we are standing in a tree-lined street but I have no idea where we are. Hayley crosses the road and jogs to the opposite bus stop but the next bus isn't due for six minutes.

"We need to get home and warn her," Hayley says. "You heard what that man said."

"Are you sure they're talking about her?" I ask.

Her face is fierce as she nods. "Who else could he

have meant?"

"How did they know?"

She glares at me for a moment, her eyes filled with suspicion and loss, then her mind turns and the expression breaks.

"It wasn't me," I say, too late.

"Of course it wasn't you," she says, almost gently. Then she pulls her arms round her chest and slumps down on to the red plastic bus stop seat. She sighs then runs her hands through her hair. "Mum said only four people knew," she says. "The guy she reports to, the station superintendent, the chief constable and the deputy director of UK Border Force."

"Nobody else?"

She shakes her head. Her knees are bouncing up and down as she urges the bus to come quicker. "They told her old department she was relocating. She isn't part of any team. They kept the whole thing especially quiet because operational details kept getting leaked to the smugglers..."

She doesn't finish her sentence.

"Do you think it could have been...?" I start, and she nods before I can finish.

"It must be one of them who's on the wrong side

and giving information across."

"Should we call the police?" I ask.

She shakes her head. "How can we? If there's someone corrupt in the force we can't let them know we know. We just need to get home and warn Mum. She'll know what to do."

And I guess she is right. I just have a horrible feeling inside that it's all my fault.

As soon as we get back, Hayley knows there is something wrong. Rachel's car is parked on the street, wedged into a space that looks impossible, and for a moment Hayley seems relieved. Until we get inside and she starts to panic.

The place looks fine to me, but Hayley knows things are not right. Rachel isn't here but her bag has been dumped on the dining table. The kettle is hot and next to it there is a cup with a tea bag in, unfilled. And the kitchen window is open.

"She nags me every time I go out to close the windows," Hayley says. "She would never leave them open. We're too late."

She sits on the sofa, with her arms wrapped round her body, rocking slightly. I stand, leaning against the wall, not knowing what to do or say. Hayley is panicking, talking wildly under her breath, blaming herself, but I tell her it's not her fault. She looks up at me sharply.

"What am I going to do?" she whispers.

I don't know what to say. I try and be practical.

"We should call the police," I say, even though every cell in my body tells me not to. Hayley nods and gets her phone. "But you can't mention Stripes," I add. "Someone your mum works with is corrupt. We can't let them know we're on to them."

And while she's on the phone I call Ronnie. "I need to talk to you," I say.

He grunts and tells me he's busy, then cuts the call, but I could hear children's TV in the background so I figure he's at home. Hayley gets off the phone and looks more upset than before.

"My mum's boss just told me not to worry," she says. "He said she was supposed to check in every two hours with him and she hadn't missed one yet. He said she probably went out in a hurry and will be back any minute."

"Did you tell him about the men we heard?"

"I couldn't," she says desperately. "What if it was

him? I couldn't tell over the phone. He might just kill her immediately. And maybe come after us."

"How long ago did she check in?"

"He said half an hour ago. That would be just before they took her. He said all we could do was wait."

But I can't just sit here. "I'm going to see Ronnie," I say. "Maybe he knows something. Do you want to come?"

She shakes her head. "I need to wait here." She crosses her arms and I see tears in her eyes. "I didn't realise how scared you must be for your dad," she says. "But now I think I do."

I nod but can't think of anything else to say. Two people both trying to do the right thing and both in serious danger for it. And it seems like we're the only ones that can help them.

I run to Ronnie's flat and bang on the door. It opens about ten centimetres and he looks mad when he sees me. But the wide-eyed face that peers out at me from behind his knees just looks curious.

He pushes the little girl back inside the flat, but she wails. I smile at her and say hello in my language. She grins and tries to say "good day" to me formally, but stumbles over the words. Ronnie yells back into the flat for someone called Ada to come and get the girl, and a beautiful young woman with large, dark eyes comes and scoops her up into her arms. She says something soothing to the girl in a language I don't recognise, then smiles at me nervously as she tries to stop the child wriggling. Ronnie turns and says something about going out. Ada asks him if he will be long. He shakes his head.

They are standing close to each other in the doorway and the little girl leans across with her arms stretched out, wanting Ronnie to take her. He doesn't want to, but the girl is determined and leans out of Ada's arms recklessly, trusting completely that he will reach out to stop her falling. She giggles when he does, then immediately turns and stretches out for the woman, who laughs and shrugs at me.

"She can be a handful," she says to me.

Ronnie tries to look angry but somehow with the girl in his arms he seems so normal it is hard to be scared of him. And I'm tired of being scared.

"She looks like you," I say to the woman. "Which is better than looking like her dad."

Ronnie looks shocked for a moment, but Ada's laugh soothes him. "Won't you come in?" she asks.

"Was it you that was here the other night?"

"Yes," I say. "Thank you for having me in your home."

Ronnie scowls but not so she can see. I make a face at the little girl, who squeals then turns her face into her mother's chest. She wriggles again and Ada soothes her.

"Come in," Ada says again. "It is time for her nap. You two talk while I settle her. Maybe you have news from home that Romek can hear."

I can tell Ronnie isn't happy but I don't care and I step into the flat. Ada takes the little girl into the other room and Ronnie sits down angrily. "You shouldn't have come to my place," he says quietly. "I gave you one night when you had nowhere else, but that was all I promised."

"I'm sorry," I say. "I didn't realise your family would be here. Is that your wife?"

"Wife?" he laughs. "How do you get married without papers? Not my wife, not my daughter. No roast beef or village green." He leans back against a wall and bites nervously at a nail. "What do you want?"

"I need to talk to you," I say. "I want you to help me."

His eyes narrow but he keeps his voice low. "I already did," he says. "I helped you on the boat and I let you stay. I give you work until you decide it is not good enough for you. You have had all my help."

"Why do you do what you do?" I ask, but he just scowls.

"I need to eat," he says. "The baby needs clothes."

"Does Ada know what you do?" I say quietly.

His eyes dart to the door to the bedroom and then back at me. "Are you going to lecture me, Little Bear?" he says. "Are you going to tell me to do right?"

"When my dad told me he was a postal worker," I say, "I didn't really know what it was. I thought everyone was something like that. Like a builder or a doctor or someone who works in a factory. What will you tell your daughter?"

He doesn't reply.

"Does Ada know what you do?" I ask again.

He shakes his head slightly.

"How would she be if she knew?"

And now anger blazes in his eyes. "Is that a threat?" he hisses, but I hold up my hands.

"No," I say. "I won't tell her. But you had a gun yesterday. Would you really shoot someone?"

He looks away and shrugs. "I have before," he says casually.

"I can read people, remember," I say. "I know you are not a murderer."

He stares at me for a moment, a strange fear sweeping over his face. "You can't always be right," he says.

"Wouldn't you like to get away from this work?" I ask. "Wouldn't it be safer?"

He stands up and walks to the window, staring out for a moment. "You can't get out from the work," he says. "They don't let you leave."

"I have met someone who might be able to help."

He turns back to me. "You meet a lot of people in two days."

"Same person."

"I don't like this conversation," he says. "You are making me nervous, Little Bear."

"You don't need to be nervous," I say, and I smile. "I can read people and I know things."

And that stops him. He hesitates. "You know nothing," he says at last.

"I know that if you stay in this life a little longer you will never get out and you will lose what you have. I know that you risked everything to come to this country, then the people who say they will help you

are the ones that trap you. I know that there is only
one way to escape the position you are in. Helping me
is the best chance for you and your family."

He looks up sharply at the word "family",
automatically raising his fingers to his mouth before
checking himself. He looks at the nails that are
bitten down, then he clenches his fist as if to stop
himself from doing more damage. He looks away past
me through the window and closes his eyes. Then
eventually he opens them again and sighs.

"So what do you think I should do?"

Before I can answer, Ada comes back in. She is
wearing brown work trousers and a cream shirt with
a name badge pinned to it. She raises her fingers to
her lips and smiles. "She didn't want to go to sleep,"
she says quietly. "She wanted to know all about the
handsome man who has the same fair hair as Daddy."
Then she looks across at Ronnie. "I need to go to
work," she says. "Are you OK with her or shall I ask Mrs
Sanchez?"

Ronnie shrugs. "What time will you finish?"

"Maybe four," she says. "I will ask for an extra shift
if I can. Do you have money for the bus?"

He nods and pulls a five-pound note from his

pocket and gives it to her. She leans down and kisses him on the forehead, then takes some keys from the table and leaves, smiling at me briefly as she closes the door.

Ronnie watches her leave then leans back in the chair. "Why should I trust this person you met?"

"They're not after people like us. They want to catch the organisers. They said they will help us if they can."

He shakes his head. "They won't help me," he says. "I need this job. How will I earn money otherwise?"

"How long before you kill someone?" I say. "Or someone dies and they need someone to blame? You are not a killer, Ronnie, I know it. I think she can help all of us."

"She?" He looks up at me and I nod. "Is it the new woman with Max? You said she was straight."

I nod again. "I didn't want you to kill her," I say. "And your boss already knew about her. He's taken her somewhere and she's going to die. So I need to know where."

He looks down. "I can't help."

"They've taken her to the boathouse," I say. "Do you know where that is?"

He doesn't answer. I take a deep breath.

"Does Ada know what you do?" I say.

"Get out of my home," he spits.

He doesn't answer. I take a deep breath.

"I could tell the others that you know she's police."

He is on his feet before the words are out. "Get out of my home before I kill you," he spits.

He doesn't answer. I take a deep breath.

"She has a daughter too," I say. "Please help me find her."

21

BEFORE

The car is dying and we don't want to get pulled over so we dump it in a public car park about thirty kilometres away from Calais and find a bus to take us into the city. As soon as we are there, we see the place is buzzing with migrants. On every street corner, in every park, on every bench, all of them, like us, desperate to get to England. Most of them look like they are from Africa or the Middle East. The young, the old, families and individuals. A man with one leg and one eye. A woman with a baby who won't stop crying. She holds it close to her and rocks back and forth on a bench that sits facing out to the sea. I wonder if she is waiting for someone, but we move on before I find out. If she is, I hope they come soon.

"Now what?" I ask Dad.

He looks as worried as I've seen him. "We need to wait for this guy Ronnie," he says. "He said he'd call."

"How much money have we got left?"

"It's going to cost almost all of it," he says, and I don't want to ask any more.

We follow a crowd of migrants to a wide space that looks like it used to be a football field but has now been turned into a makeshift meeting point. A large dirty white Toyota pickup is parked on one side of the space, and two French women stand on the back, handing out bottles of water. Nearby, a tent has been erected marked with a red cross where people can get medical attention and already the queue has thirty people in it. We stand to the side and try and work out what to do but now that we have arrived it seems we have no idea what comes next. We stand still in the dusty air trying to get the hang of the place, until eventually I notice a boy about my age standing on the edge of the field watching us.

He is dressed in dirty jeans and a torn French football shirt and holding a crumpled piece of pale-blue paper in his hand. I nod at him but instead of looking back he just glances at the paper again, then turns quickly and runs off to speak to a group of men. They start talking and looking in our direction. There is something wrong. I grab Dad's arm and march him away.

"They were staring at us," I say. "That boy had a piece of paper." And then I see something similar crumpled on the ground. "Like this one," I add. And when I pick it up I almost freeze with horror. It is Dad's picture with a message in French and English underneath it. *"Call this number,"* it says. *"Get a reward of ten thousand euros."*

The colour drains from Dad's face. When I look around I can see lots of these flyers fluttering about, littering the ground. He puts his head down and we walk away until we find a quiet spot in the middle of some trees. He takes out his phone and checks it again. And at last there is a message.

"He's sending a boy called Hassam to meet us," Dad says. "By the aid station."

"Give him my description and tell him I'll be there in ten minutes. Stay out of sight and I'll be back soon."

I don't wait for him to argue, and hurry off back to the tent. Everywhere I look the blue pieces of paper are blowing around in the breeze and when I reach the football pitch my heart almost stops. Standing in the middle of the scrubby grass is Corporal Tritzin, one of the soldiers who came to our house.

He is standing between me and the tent, holding a thick pile of the blue flyers, giving them to anyone who will take one. As I walk past, he offers one to me but I just keep going with my head down. He doesn't seem to recognise me and turns to hand one to someone else. There are hundreds of these flyers and we are surrounded by desperate people. It is only a matter of time before someone says they've seen us.

I get to the tent and try to blend into the crowd but most of the migrants seem to be from Syria or Africa and don't look like me. After five minutes I notice a man of about twenty staring at me and I take a chance.

"Hassam?" I say, and when he nods I feel like I can breathe again.

He instructs me in broken English to follow him but I tell him we have to get my dad first. He says to hurry, but he didn't need to. I almost run back to Dad and reach him just as he is finishing a phone call, but before I can ask him who he's calling, Hassam points at Dad then pulls another blue flyer from his pocket.

"You!" he says, pointing at Dad.

Dad laughs and shakes his head but it is clear Hassam has recognised him. I grab the piece of paper from his hand and screw it up before throwing it away. "You need to take us to Ronnie," I say quickly. "He's waiting for us."

Hassam hesitates then nods. He tells us to leave our bags then leads us through the trees away from the field until we get to a chain fence. He points to a hole that has been cut and urges us through, waving at us to hurry across empty roads until we are in front of a large warehouse, where finally he bangs on the door and runs off.

We wait for minutes, but each one seems like a year until eventually the door opens and a man appears. He is dressed in jeans and a white shirt under a black jacket and has short blond hair. The head of a dragon tattoo curls out of the top of his shirt and his expression is fierce.

"Are you Ronnie?" Dad asks.

"You got the money?"

"Yes."

"Give it to me."

Dad counts out eight thousand euros but as he holds out the last note Ronnie's face turns hard.

"We said pounds," Ronnie says.

Dad's eyes widen. "It's all I've got."

I pull at Dad's sleeve. "I've still got Grandmother's jewellery," I say in our own language, but when I do Ronnie spins and stares at me.

"Where are you from?" Ronnie says in the same language.

I stare at him. "The same place as you, maybe," I say.

He holds my gaze for a moment before holding out his hand and I put the necklace and earrings into it. He turns them over in his palm, then seems to think. He nods at Dad and tells him to wait while he pulls a blue piece of paper out of his pocket. He unfolds it and stares at it before staring at Dad.

"This is you," he says, and my stomach feels like it's going to drop out of my body.

I turn back to Dad. "We've got to go," I say, but before he can move, Ronnie reaches out and pulls Dad hard through the door. I rush at him but his grip is too strong and now he yanks us both inside.

"You are worth ten thousand euros," he hisses. "Do you think they will let you go for nothing?"

But before Dad can respond another boy rushes up and tells Ronnie the truck is coming.

Dad stares at Ronnie. "We should talk about this," he says. "There's things you don't know."

But Ronnie shakes his head. "These things are not my decision."

"Then I need to speak to whoever's decision it is!"

Ronnie hesitates then nods quickly. He beckons us deeper inside the dark warehouse and tells us to stand against the metal wall. All around us faces stare through the gloom; hundreds of men, women and children, huddled together in the dark.

Another man rushes up and repeats that the truck is outside. Ronnie nods. "Start loading them up," he says. Then he points at me. "Him too."

Dad looks like he's about to tell me to get on the truck but there's no way I'm going without him and he knows it. Outside, we hear the sound of a lorry and the men start shouting orders at the migrants to line up. Men in one line, women in another and children separate. Women scream that they need to be with their children but the smugglers don't care. Unless they are small, the children go separate. When I tell them I'm not getting on until Dad gets back, Ronnie grimaces but seems to accept it. He orders me to wait quietly and tells me I will be shot if I try anything.

As Dad turns to go, he catches my eye deliberately and his head tips in a very slight nod. For a moment I wonder what he means and then I realise he is telling me to use my gift to stay alert. My heart is already racing but now a strange new feeling sweeps through me. Maybe he is starting to accept the gift I have. Maybe he is starting to accept me. I nod back and see a grim smile spread across his mouth.

Until Ronnie grabs his arm and they both disappear into the gloom.

22

AFTER

Ronnie leans back in the chair and rubs his face with his hands. "I would like to get married," he says quietly. "I have done bad things, but I never thought I was bad. I wanted to be a train driver but you can't drive a train without papers." He looks at his hands then scrunches them into fists as if to hide the damage. "You really think your woman can help me?" he says.

I nod. "She's part of the system. She said she could."

He sighs. "I know where the boathouse is," he says. "I will show you on a map. Are you going to go there?"

"I don't know. Maybe the police will."

He nods. "It is where we meet before we go to France," he says. "And where they keep the passports."

"What passports?"

He raises a hand to his mouth unconsciously, then thinks better of it and lowers it again. "If you need work they say you can work for them but they take your passport," he says. "And if you have no passport, you can't ask for help and you can't go home. It is their insurance so nobody talks."

"Have they got your passport?"

He nods.

"And Ada's?"

He nods again. "They say they will destroy them all

if there is a raid," he says. "And if they do that I am nothing."

I look around the room at the drawings and the toys. "You are not nothing," I say. "You are a brother and a son and a partner. And you are a father."

He smiles at the words, but then he shakes his head. "You don't know what I've done," he says. "Your father—" he starts, but then he stops.

And I can feel the fear growing inside me.

"What about him?"

"All he cared about was keeping you safe."

"So?"

"Your dad was hurt on the beach." he begins, then he hesitates. "He told me to leave him and look after you."

I stare at him in horror. "Is he dead?"

Ronnie shrugs. "I don't know. But if he is alive he is still in France."

I feel a pain like my heart is on fire. If he is alive either the smugglers have got him or he is hiding somewhere but I can't remember what happened and I just wish the memories were not so messed up in my mind. And if he is injured or held, maybe the only chance I've got is getting Rachel free so she can help him somehow. I call Hayley from outside Ronnie's flat and tell her the boathouse is in a place called Shoreham. And my heart sinks when she tells me there's no news from Rachel.

"If Mum hasn't called by the time you get here, we'll go and have a look," she says. And when I get to the house she is by the door ready to go.

It takes us twenty minutes to get to the small town of Shoreham and every minute feels like we're going to be too late. Hayley sits in the back of the taxi with her phone in her hand, urging it to ring but it doesn't. Eventually the car stops near an old-fashioned lighthouse, which the map on my phone says is two minutes' walk away. We get out and I suddenly feel exposed.

"Are you sure you want to do this?" I ask, but there is no doubt in Hayley's eyes. "Do you want to try the police again?" I say, but she shakes her head.

"No," she says. "I don't trust the guy I spoke to. He said he would call me back if he heard anything. Better to let them think I'm not worried."

We walk along the side of a road next to a wide estuary that runs into the sea, then follow a path that runs down to our left towards the water, to an underpass where a number of small fishing businesses and boat-related operations line up along the bank. At the end of the path is a single, battered Range Rover and space for three more cars, and beyond that a large, filthy blue building that juts out slightly over the dirty water. The paint is peeling off the ten-metre-high corrugated iron walls and at first glance it looks like it was abandoned years ago. But as we get closer I notice what looks like a new alarm system flashing on the rear wall.

We stop outside a shop that sells parts for boat motors; a dirty, sprawling mess of a place with plenty of engine parts but no people to be seen, just a sign saying the owners will be back in ten minutes. Hayley points at a gap down the side of the workshop and leads me down a small path to a scrubby patch of grass where a chain-link fence guards the back of the boathouse.

"How are we going to get in?" I whisper, but when I turn to Hayley she has gone back to the workshop next door. She returns a few seconds later heaving a greasy-looking tool kit, which she opens, taking out a set of wire cutters. Then she points to the back of the boathouse and beckons me forward. We crouch down and move forward as fast as we can until we are at the fence. No one has seen us.

It takes a few moments to cut the wire and once we are in I feel less exposed. It doesn't look as if anyone comes round to the back of the building as the ground is scattered with old equipment, a few pallets and about twenty years' worth of litter. There is a row of what looks like office windows about four metres up but if we stay close to the side no one can see us. And we can clearly hear the throb of engines and occasional snatches of shouted conversations from inside.

When I tug at a loose piece of the rusting iron wall it comes away in my fingers so I try again and this time a large piece bends and separates, leaving my hand covered in orange filth. Hayley sees what I am doing and starts copying me, working away around the hole until there is a space big enough to see through, then we lie flat on the ground, silently staring into the huge space in front of us. The hole comes out below a table of some kind and in front of us a smooth concrete floor runs away for about twenty metres before it reaches the water with two boats pulled up on the sides of the dock. Somewhere above our heads a radio is playing, and on one of the boats someone in dirty jeans is singing along while they move in and out of the small cabin.

But there is no sign of Rachel.

I roll away from the hole in the wall, lying on my back for a moment, staring at the sky.

"She must be in the offices above," I say. "We need to make a ladder out of those pallets so we can see in the windows."

Hayley nods and we grab a pallet and lean it against the rear wall, but it is still not high enough so we get another one and rest it on top of the first. It is hard to stay silent and my heart is pounding but the radio seems to be covering some of the noise and nobody comes. I am about to climb up to look through the windows but Hayley beats me to it. I press the pallets against the wall to keep them steady until she reaches the window.

"There's no sign of Mum, but this window's pretty rusty," she whispers. "I think I can open it."

I concentrate on keeping the pallets still while she takes a screwdriver and jams it into the window frame. Shards of rust shower down on to my head before there is a creaking sound and the window pops open. Hayley forces it wider, then slides herself over the ledge, leaning out a second later to hold the pallet still while I climb up.

But just as I get through the window, the pallets crash down to the ground.

The sound rings out through the air and vibrates through the metal walls.

I dive headfirst into the small office and look around. There is a desk with a computer on it in front of a wooden filing cabinet. On the side is a large old wardrobe, which I run and open. It is full of bright-yellow waterproof clothing and sailing gear with just about enough room for us to hide in.

I grab Hayley's hand and pull her to the wardrobe, forcing her inside and clambering in after her, just as the office door opens.

We freeze as someone comes into the room.

"Nothing in here," he shouts, and I almost breathe out before he stops. "Hold on," he says. "There's a window open."

I feel Hayley tense next to me and can almost hear her heart pounding. We are crushed together awkwardly and the arm I am leaning on is screaming with pain. The man moves slowly and now I can see Hayley's eyes widen as she realises all of her weight is on my arm too. I start to count in my head as a distraction from the pain, getting to six before we hear the window creak and the man slams it shut. I clench my teeth to stop myself screaming and keep counting. *Ten, eleven, twelve,* until eventually we hear him speak again.

"Some rubbish has blown over in the wind," he says but he still doesn't go. "Maybe we should get these windows sorted," he adds. And then finally he leaves the room.

I roll out of the cupboard and lie on the floor, panting hard, my eyes screwed shut as I rub my arm until the pain slowly ebbs away. Hayley stares at me anxiously but I tell her I'm fine.

Then I tell her to wait while I go and look around.

I open the office door and dart out as quickly as I can on to a narrow landing that overlooks the boathouse. To my left are stairs down to ground level, where I can see the man who is doing something with the engine. To my right the landing leads on to a closed door, which has the key in the lock. I march along fast, not caring about being seen, and unlock the door. Inside, Rachel is tied to a chair, tape across her mouth. Her eyes widen as she sees me and she tries to say something through the tape but it just comes out as a muffled groan. I place my fingers on my lips and look around the room. It seems to be a meeting room, with a table that has been pushed to the side and chairs piled up against the back wall. I go to the window and open it. We can get out but there is a load of metal rubbish below, which would be dangerous to jump on to, and it would be much easier to get out downstairs. I leave the room again and walk back, pausing on the landing to scan the area below. The stairs lead down to the main workspace and the doors are on the left. The only person I can see is the man working on the boat but I can hear someone moving around below the stairs. I don't know how long I have had, but it feels like I'm getting to the end of my time. I yell out, "Come and see me," as loud as I can. There is a sound of something being dropped and the other person runs out into the main space to stare up at me. It is Stripes.

I look up at Hayley.

"Your mum's in the next office along," I say. "She's tied up and gagged. There are two men here, both

214

downstairs. And I don't see any way out unless we go past them."

She stares at me, and I realise what I have done.

"How do you know?" she asks in a whisper. "How can you possibly know that?"

I don't know what to say. "This isn't the time," I say. "I'll tell you but not now."

But that isn't enough for her. "Have you been here before?" she asks. "Are you part of this?" She stares at me with fire in her eyes. "Are you one of them?"

I shake my head. "No," I insist. "But there really isn't time. We need to get your mum out and then I'll tell you."

And I don't wait for her to argue. I just open the door and march out.

When we open the door Rachel's eyes widen in shock and then relief as we untie her. But there is no time for talking. I check there is no one about and then we creep back into the other room and close the door behind us. Rachel looks out of the window.

"OK," she says. "We can get out if we hang down from the window ledge and drop. It's a metre or two but it's not too far."

Hayley nods and climbs up, then spins on the edge

and backs out of the window gracefully, hanging for a moment before pushing herself away from the wall and dropping down the two metres on to the grass. She rolls as she lands, then stands up and waves that she's OK. Rachel turns for me to go next, but I am busy.

There is nowhere else in the meeting room or this office so I figure the filing cabinet must be where they keep the passports, but when I try to open it I can't. I pull hard at the door, expecting the lock to be small and breakable but it doesn't budge, and when I look at it I can tell it is designed for higher security than a standard office.

"What the hell are you doing?" Rachel hisses, but I wave her away.

"You go," I say. "I promised someone I'd get their passport back. I think it must be in here but it's locked."

"Leave it," she whispers. "We'll come back and get it."

But I shake my head. "Just go," I say. "I'll be right behind you."

But she doesn't. I can hear Hayley outside, telling us to hurry, but the lock just won't move. I find a pair of scissors and try and jam that into it, but it does no good. I stare around the room, but I can't think of anything else. Rachel is getting more frantic.

"These guys are killers," she whispers. "If you don't get out now, I'm going to throw you out."

And that's the answer.

"Help me," I urge, grabbing the cabinet and tipping it so I can drag it across the room. She stares at me for a moment then helps me get it to the window and lift it up. I wave at Hayley to get out of the way, then lever it up on to the sill and push it out hard. It falls to the ground and crashes into the pallets, shattering. As I swing myself out after it and drop down I can see the passports and papers have spilled out on to the grass below, but there are loads of them and the papers are in a real mess.

I start to rummage through them, but it takes several seconds to go through just a few and I am not going fast enough. Rachel drops down beside me as I get to fifteen seconds but I ignore her and keep going frantically until I find Ada's black passport. My head feels like it's going to explode and I am beyond where I thought I could be but there are still passports all over the grass, tangled up in papers and in the wreckage of the cabinet. It is taking too long. "Just pick them

217

up," whispers Rachel. *It is the only thing to do, and I can't steal any more time to do it.*

I pick Ada's passport from the pile and shove it in my pocket then start rummaging through the rest of the mess, picking out all the others that I can see. Rachel drops down beside me and I urge her to do the same. Hayley runs back from the fence. She doesn't understand what's going on and tries to drag Rachel away, but she won't leave without me. And I won't leave without Ronnie's passport. I kick aside the wreckage of the cabinet and more spill out. There is one more the same colour as mine and I grab it urgently and shove it in my pocket with Ada's. Rachel has also got a pile in her arms and there don't seem to be any more that could be right. She stoops to pick up another one, but I tell her it's time to go.

Finally we run to the gap in the fence and start to crawl through.

Just as Stripes appears. He is holding a gun and pointing it right at us.

"I think you'd better stop where you are," he says.

And we have no choice but to do what he says.

23

BEFORE

Dad and Ronnie leave while I watch them load the migrants into the truck. Men, then women, then children into the gaps so that the lorry is packed with more people than I thought possible.

And as soon as the smugglers are busy, I run off after them, down the side of the building to a door with a glass window where I can see Ronnie. He is right in front of the window but I can just make out Dad inside the room, sitting at a table, opposite another man who I can't see except for his short grey hair. They are talking about something but I can't hear. I need to get in but I don't know how. I twist the door handle and shove it hard but it hits Ronnie and now he turns angrily.

There is no way I can get in. And I don't know what they are talking about.

I wait for Dad to come back, feeling the blood pounding in my veins for every second. He looks determined, but stern-faced.

"What's going on?" I say, but he doesn't answer. He just tells me that if we get separated I should stay with Ronnie. His words are like a stab of dread inside me, but I force it away. Because we're not going to get separated, are we?

The truck is loaded now and we scramble on to the back, between the crush of bodies. One of Ronnie's men shouts to hurry, because they will miss the tides, but Ronnie doesn't seem to be in any rush. And seconds later I know what they're waiting for. Because the warehouse door opens again. And framed in the doorway is Corporal Tritzin.

Panic floods through me and we slam ourselves out of sight against the side of the truck. Ronnie tells one of his men to make sure no one gets off the lorry, then walks up to the soldier and speaks to him briefly. Then they both walk off towards the office.

"Ronnie promised we could go," Dad whispers. "But he's scared of the main guy. I don't trust them."

The warehouse door is still open and about twenty metres away. "They've double-crossed you," I whisper back. "We need to get out of here. If we run we might make it."

Dad shakes his head. "We need to get to England. The only way is on this lorry."

But if we stay where we are we are trapped.

The driver leans out of his window and yells at Ronnie that they need to go to meet the boat. "The landing point's twenty-five kilometres down the coast," he shouts. "Unless we go soon we will miss the tide."

Ronnie barks at him to keep quiet then rushes off to check what's going on. But he'll be back any second.

"We need to get off," I hiss. "We'll run out and find a place to get back on outside."

Dad nods, pushing to the front and jumping down before I can look forward. He jumps straight into the man guarding the lorry, catching him by surprise and knocking him off his feet. And before he can respond we are running for the door.

Behind us, somebody yells and I hear the sound of feet hitting the floor hard, but I don't turn round. Dad slams his shoulder into the door and we burst out into the night. The smugglers are right behind us, but now it is dark and we are sprinting so they don't catch us. We tear along the side of the warehouse, down a path that leads out on to some of the main roads. Ahead I can see a busy road where we might be able to lose ourselves in the crowd, but Dad grabs my arm and we lurch to the side, down a small lane that doubles back on where we have been. After another hundred metres the lane dwindles to a footpath with bushes on either side and we dive into them and lie still, panting hard.

A few seconds later several of the smugglers appear at the end of the path and go past, followed almost immediately by Tritzin. He is furious, screaming at them to find us, until Ronnie comes up beside him and tells him to keep his voice down. Then he tells his men to get back to the truck. Tritzin says something harsh about a deal, but Ronnie tells him to shut up in our language and pulls a gun out of his waistband. He looks at his watch and tells Tritzin they need to get back. Tritzin tells him to think about the money but Ronnie tells him to shut up again. And then the boss arrives.

His voice is deep and quiet and I have to strain to hear, but he takes charge instantly. He tells Ronnie to get back then stands face to face with Tritzin. "You will still get your man," he says in whispered English.

"He needs to go tonight," Tritzin says harshly.

"My boat is the only one tonight," the man says but Tritzin shakes his head.

"I don't trust you," he whispers. "Why is your man Ronnie so keen to help them?"

"Ronnie will do what I tell him. If you don't believe me come to the beach with us and see. But that will mean your price goes up when I do catch him."

Tritzin grunts. "Money is not a problem," he says. "But I ride up front. I'm not going in the back with those refugees."

The man laughs. "Fine," he says. "But we need to go. We have to get the tide."

Dad and I wait a full minute then crawl out of the bushes. Silently, not speaking; scared but determined. When we get to the end of the path I ask Dad if he wants me to look ahead. He hesitates slightly then nods.

"You don't need to ask," he says. "Make good decisions and give us all the help you can."

I jog up the road to the warehouse, as quietly as I can, clinging to the edges of the buildings until I reach the door but my time is almost up. I stand by the corner of the warehouse as I get to fifteen seconds. I hear the engine of the lorry rev...

"We can get to the corner," I say. "Then the lorry is going to come out. We are just going to have to take a chance."

Dad nods. "Are you sure you want to?" he says.

"We've got no choice," I say. And there is no time for anything more.

We run up the road to the corner of the warehouse, just as the lorry reverses out and the rear swings round. As it turns, there is a moment when the driver is leaning out of his window and everyone is watching the left side of the truck so it does not hit one of the bollards outside.

"Now," Dad barks, and we run out, staying on the right, aiming for the gap between the cab and the container. Dad scrambles on and finds a hold on a pipe that rises up behind the cab. I lean forward to grab it too, but the truck has started moving again and I have to jog to keep up. Panic sweeps through me as I can't find anything to hold and I can't grab Dad because it might drag him off. The lorry moves faster and I am sprinting, falling behind as it goes forward. I push as fast as I can, forcing my legs to move, then leap just as Dad has settled himself. He turns and catches me, his strong hands wrapping round my arm and clinging to my jacket. He hauls me up beside him and we perch precariously in the tiny gap as the lorry accelerates away at speeds that we won't recover from if we fall.

"You're OK," he whispers. "I've got you. We just need to hold on for as long as we can."

24

AFTER

Stripes recognises us from the house but it doesn't seem to bother him. In fact he seems pleased that he's managed to tie up a loose end. I think about trying to rush at him to escape, but he is too careful. He stands several metres away, always with the gun trained on us, while the mechanic tapes our hands together and drags us upstairs. Even if I could run, it would leave Rachel and Hayley and I won't do that. I try and think of a way to use the seconds I have but I can't. There is nothing to do except wait.

They put us in the office and tape us firmly to chairs so that we can't move, then tear off more strips of tape to put over our mouths. Just before they gag me I scream at Stripes to tell me if he knows about my dad. He doesn't understand at first, then the shock registers as he works out who I am. I urge him to tell me what he knows but he just shrugs.

"One of the men on the beach died," he says bluntly. "And we dumped the body on the way back, but I don't know if it was your dad." He hesitates. "People die trying to get across," he adds. "We don't make them do it."

I yell at him to tell me more, but that's all he'll say. I try and get up, straining against my bonds, but he just nods at the mechanic, who sticks the tape on my mouth, then turns to go. We hear his steps pause on the landing while he makes a call.

"Those kids from the house just turned up," he says. "It's her daughter and the son of that guy from the beach. They used the filing cabinet to smash a window trying to get her out." He listens for a moment, then he sounds almost sad. "I don't like it," he says, "but I guess we don't have much choice, do we?" Another pause. "Fine. Be easier to do it here and dump the bodies later but I guess you know more about evidence than me. Ronnie will do what he's told. We'll do it when we're halfway across." He pauses again. "We're leaving in four hours. See you in France." Then we hear the heavy tramp of his shoes down the stairs, and after that there is nothing.

We are taped up in three chairs, facing away from each other, unable to move or talk. There is nothing to do except sit in fear but after some time even that drifts away. I think about Dad and try to remember what happened on the beach but it is too hazy and the dread of what might have happened to him fades as the hours roll by. Rachel and Hayley communicate a little with grunts and looks but eventually they stop moving too. The world is silent and still and I am literally locked in place. For a while my head spins until the time dulls it and fills it with the empty afternoon. I do the only thing I can think of, and practise.

And the time just flies. I can't do anything or look at anything or hear anything. All I can do is keep the world still and feel the time go by. I notice the dust floating in the air and I notice how certain it is that it will fall. I notice the breeze blowing through the grass on the bank behind the building and how the grass must ripple as the wind blows. I watch as a small beetle crawls its way across the floor, evenly and inevitably. Slowly, deliberately and inevitably; moving to the other side of the room, maybe in seconds or minutes or hours, I can't tell which, but I know perfectly in advance where it is going and where it has come from. I watch its life unfold before my eyes and finally I think I can start to grasp what Grandmother was trying to tell me.

"Take the time to practise," she said, and at last I understand what she meant. She didn't mean "Find the time". She meant "Take the time". I have all the time in the world to practise because I can take it and use it. A few seconds at first but if I use it I can build it up until it is longer and then I can use that to practise too. I almost laugh but I don't want to disturb the moment. "Take the time to practise," she said, and now I have all the time I need. I run through the exercises again and again, watching the little creature move forward but never getting closer as I loop the time in my head and concentrate harder than I have ever done before.

"You can watch and you can see and you can know," she said. "You can't change the future but you can see what is coming and change the present." And now I see it stretching out for seconds and minutes and hours.

The beetle reaches the other wall. Stripes comes back into the room. He forces us to get up. He forces us on to the boat. The gun will be pointed at us. And it will fire...

I pause. There are stories of someone who can take all the time in the world, she said, and now I know why. Because if you can take a second you can take another second in the time it takes for the first. And if you can do that you can take a minute or an hour or a day. And if you have fifteen seconds to start with, the whole future is yours to see. You just need a chance to see it.

I run it again, almost thrilled at what I can do, but horrified at the result.

They come into the room and drag us out.

It is the only path to follow, unless I change it, and I wonder what would happen then. If I change the present and follow a new path, where would that lead? I stretch out and try to see...

The door opens at last. Rachel flinches and tries to turn so she is facing it. Stripes is there and he has the gun in his hand. "Time to go," he says. "One at a time. I'm going to take you down to the boat and we're going to hop across to France." Tears run down Hayley's face and he stares at them for a moment, before turning away. "You first," he says to Rachel. "Let's get going."

He points the gun at her while the mechanic cuts away her bonds, but he doesn't remove the tape from her mouth. She stands, a little shakily at first, twisting to find Hayley's eyes with hers before she is dragged away.

Two minutes later they come back for me. They force me to follow them down the stairs to where a small fishing boat is being prepared to leave, then shove me roughly into the cabin. It is a gloomy space with worn wooden panelling and a small bench that wraps round a plastic-topped table but there is no sign of Rachel. As I scan the small room, I notice a door at the side, which I stare at as they tie me to the single metal leg of the table. Stripes sees me looking and shakes his head.

"Don't let the others know what's down here," he tells the mechanic. "And keep the kids separated from the woman. Keep her locked in the bathroom until it's time."

"What if we need to use it?" the mechanic asks, but Stripes just glares at him.

"You're at sea at night," he says. "Use your imagination!"

Two minutes later they bring down Hayley and dump her on the seat next to me, then tie her up so that we are sitting close together facing into the cabin. They close the doors and everything goes dark. Then they leave us alone.

There is not much we can do. I have taken all the time I need and the only way forward on this path leads to failure, but I refuse to give up trying. If I twist my head, I can touch the wooden wall with my face and I rub repeatedly against it to loosen the tape against my mouth. The dirty surface is rough against my cheek, but eventually a thread comes loose, and then another one. Hayley works out what I'm doing and tries to do the same thing, but there is not enough room for us both to try so we take it in turns. I still haven't made much progress when we hear the hum of the boat's motor and the throb, which reverberates throughout the boat. The rise and fall of the water becomes more pronounced and then we are moving. A little more light spills in through the grimy portholes as they open the boathouse doors, then full daylight as we move out into the estuary and power out towards the sea.

Men on the boat speak to each other but it is too muffled to tell how many there are. And when they show no sign of checking on us, we increase the pace of our movements. Hayley has a scratch on her cheek that is bleeding freely but she moves frantically, ignoring the pain, until eventually the corner of the tape on her mouth folds over. She keeps working at it, using the stickiness to gain traction and now it moves faster. Eventually it hangs free and she turns to me, leaning down so she can stretch out and bite the tape away from my face. I wince as it rips away from my lips and mouth but it feels like a victory. And we need everything we can get right now.

We sit there panting at the exertion. But at last we can talk. She asks about Rachel with panic in her voice, but I manage to calm her. I gesture towards the door and tell her she's OK. But I don't know how long for.

"Maybe we can get our hands free," she says, "if we work together."

But we can't. It is impossible to reach round behind our backs to get at the bonds and eventually we have to give up.

"How long do you think we've got?" she says, and I know the answer already.

"Maybe a couple of hours," I say, and I start to tell her not to worry but she cuts me off. She stares at me in the gloom with a fierce expression on her face.

"Right," she says. "It's time to start talking."

25

BEFORE

We can't hold on for long. We are perched on a thin metal grille in the narrow space between the cab and the container and every time the lorry makes a sharp turn we have to slide across so we are not crushed between the two. Below us, the black road surface occasionally flashes with the white of road lines or markings, but all that does is give a sense of how fast we're going. Fumes seem to swirl around us and I feel sick almost immediately, but if I fall off I know I will die. The lorry shakes violently and twice my fingers slip from the grip I have taken against the mudguards over the wheels. I scramble off my jacket then use the arms to tie it to a metal tube that is sticking up from the back of the cab so at least now there is something easier to hold on to and I can relax a little. Dad does the same, then we sit as still as we can and hope that the journey will finish soon.

But it doesn't. It seems to go on for hours. On bigger roads at first then smaller roads with sharper bends, and potholes that almost hurl us out below the wheels. Pain rips through my legs as cramp grips my body and when we stop at a junction I feel like I have to move so I don't scream in agony. Then the lorry lurches off again and I throw myself down to hold on. Dad's arm jabs out and grabs my elbow and I let him take my weight briefly before I settle myself and the journey resumes. I can practically taste the diesel and now Dad is holding my arm I can lean my head out of the side to feel the fresh wind rush over my face. I gasp with relief, and when I turn to look back at him I can see Dad is grinning.

"What?" I yell over the noise of the engine.

"You were smiling," he says.

"You try it!"

We get to a long straight part of the road and I hold him and he leans out too. Then we lock our arms in a tight grip, hand to wrist, and both ride along with our heads sticking out of the sides of the lorry until it feels like we're flying. For a short time all the madness of the last days is forgotten. I whoop into the black night and look across as Dad does the same. We howl out in unison, and in this instant I wish I could stay like this forever, laughing and howling and flying like we are invincible because we are together. But the moment fades too soon. The truck slows for a bend and the roar of the engine dies so we crouch down into our nest behind the cab and retreat back into the real world.

"I love you, Alex," he says quietly. "I wish I said it more."

"I love you too, Dad," I say back, and it feels like I never really knew what it meant before now. Then the time is gone as the engine roars and the lorry lurches forward. And the journey resumes once more.

Eventually the lorry slows and then stops, waiting with its lights off. Cab doors open and men get out, moving quickly and hissing whispered instructions. I jump down and roll under the lorry, grabbing Dad as he jumps down after me, watching to see what happens now, not sure if there is still a place on the boat for us. Close by, I can hear the roar of the sea and the air is full of the tang of salt but there is nothing else to see or hear. Everything is pitch dark until one of the smugglers turns on a torch and walks quickly round to the back of the truck. We crawl between the wheels until we emerge at the back where Ronnie is opening the rear doors.

And Tritzin steps into the small beam of light.

He is standing a few metres away, watching as Ronnie cranks the lever and the door swings open. A relieved moan rises up from the people crammed

RUNNiNG
OUT OF TIME

inside the metal box, but it is short-lived and soon turns into shouts of frustration. Ronnie snaps at the migrants to shut up, hissing in several languages that the police will come if they make a noise, and eventually they calm. Then he starts letting them off the truck one by one, so that Tritzin can check their faces as they leave. He sends them down a small path towards the sea. To where the boat is waiting.

We lie still as the mass of people slowly leave the truck, but I can feel the tension rising within me.

"We need to get into the crowd," I hiss to Dad, and I can just make out the faint movement as he nods. We scramble to the very back of the truck, until we can see the feet of the migrants as they balance on the edge of the container, before jumping down on to the road. Some wait to take a hand offered to help them down but most drop, relieved to be out of the blackness and the heat of the metal container. They pause as the soldier looks at them then waves them through and they disappear into the darkness.

"You go first. I'll distract them," I hiss, but Dad shakes his head. "It's OK," I say. "You need to trust me. I can do enough seconds. I can see if it will work. When you're near the front I'll distract them so you can go through."

He stares at me, his face rigid with indecision. "It's too dangerous for you," he says. "It's me they're after. You go first. If they stop me you carry on."

He moves out of the way so I can roll under the truck but I grab his shirt. "No, Dad," I insist. "I've got this. Trust me and we'll both get through."

But again his eyes are full of doubt. "You are the greatest gift I've ever had and I'm sorry I never told you," he whispers. "I love you and I always will."

And then he pulls himself out of my grip and pushes me out from under the lorry.

I want to scream and turn back, but all I can do is scramble to my feet and join the line as if I've just jumped down. The man in front of me turns slightly, the whites of his eyes shining wide towards me, but he doesn't say anything. The lorry is parked on the road at the top of a cliff and the sea roars out in front of us. Further along the coast I can see the lights of a small village, but there are no buildings near us and no indication that there is anyone around. I am desperate to turn and look for Dad but Tritzin is only metres away, at the top of a small path that leads down the cliff to the sea below. He is watching us carefully and there is no way down without going past him. And now there are only three people between him and me. All I can do is hunch my shoulders and stare at the ground, limping slightly and coughing so I can keep my hand in front of my face. Two more people go past and now I am in front of them. Tritzin flashes the torch at me then waves me impatiently forward.

He is looking for a man, not a boy. I am not important.

One of the smugglers watches as we walk down a series of steps that are cut into the cliff face. The migrants walk down slowly, reaching out to the rock to manage the steep descent in the pitch dark, but I can't stop yet. Round a bend I can hear another of the smugglers urge the migrants to hurry, but he can't see me and now Tritzin is behind us too so I stop and look back. It is hard to see anything more than the brief flash of the torch as the migrants pass the checkpoint and I have no idea when Dad will reach him. I just flatten myself against the stone wall and try to control my breathing.

I have fifteen seconds but I don't know how to use it.

I start back up the narrow path, pushing myself

quickly against the tide of migrants but it takes too long and I reach Tritzin just as Dad does. He walks confidently then turns as if to say something to his neighbour. He starts walking past the soldier and for a moment I feel the rush of relief as I think he's made it. But he hasn't. Tritzin seems to think for a second then he puts out his hand to stop Dad. Dad raises his hand against the glare of the light, but Tritzin tells him to put it down. For a moment the two men...

And I have no more time.

I run back up the path as fast as I can but a woman barges into me in the darkness and we both fall. I spring to my feet and sprint the last few metres, just in time to see Dad reach Tritzin. He looks confident and turns to say something to his neighbour, but it plays out like I know it will. Tritzin tells him to put down his hand and stares at him. For a moment the two men look at each other. And then Tritzin takes a step back and reaches for his weapon.

I crash into him, knocking the torch from his hand. It hits the ground hard and we are plunged into darkness. I feel his arm grab at me, but I am up too quickly, reaching for Dad's shoulder then pulling him towards the path down to the sea. We shove our way through the line of people and just reach the top as new torch beams pierce the darkness around us. We charge down the steps, past the frightened bodies, forcing our way through, ignoring the smuggler who is halfway down. Shouts rise behind us, quickly followed by urgent calls for silence, then the heavy sounds of footsteps down the steps. We turn sharply as we get to the bottom and now I feel sand under my feet. I am still holding Dad's arm and he catches me as I stumble on the soft ground. The sea roars in my ears but all I can see is the flash of a torch beam ahead and the back of the migrant in front of me walking towards it.

"This way," whispers Dad, and we lurch off to the right, running hard across the beach until the sand dunes hide us from everyone behind. We collapse to the ground then turn to look back where we came from.

Dad lies next to me, panting. "Why did you do that?" he hisses. "I was just about to go through."

"No you weren't," I say. "He was just about to catch you. I saw it, Dad. I knew what was going to happen."

Now we are on the open beach the light is better. The wind whips a spray of salt water over us and moves the clouds so that moonlight occasionally reflects off the sea and silhouettes the figures as they move across the sand. Ahead of us the line of migrants stretches out from the cliff path across the sand out to the water. About twenty metres into the sea, a small fishing boat bobs on the water, the faint beam of a torch guiding the stream of people towards it through the night, but I don't see how they can all get on. It is a small boat and there must be a hundred people. One of the smugglers is directing them, his voice echoing through the darkness. Children at the front of the boat. Adults at the back. The weight has to be even, he says in English. Only then will the boat be safe.

Several of the torch beams come together in front of the boat about thirty metres away from us and I recognise Tritzin's long coat as he talks briefly, then turns and stands between us and the boat. His hand hangs down by his side and I wonder why. Until a torch beam catches it and I notice the glint of metal from the gun he is holding. I turn on to my back.

"What do you want to do?" I whisper.

Dad hesitates. For a moment, the moon comes out from behind a cloud and I see the expression on his face. His gaze flicks between the boat and the soldier and his eyes are full of doubt.

"I don't know," he says.

Behind us the beach goes on for what looks like miles, with the tall cliff on our right and small lights of a village or town in the distance. In front of us the people are getting on the boat in a brutally efficient operation, organised perfectly to squeeze as much life as possible on to a ten-metre float of fibreglass and wood. I watch as the white deck is slowly filled with people and hear the order to move up so more can get on. Tritzin ignores it as he patrols between us and the water. The smugglers want silence, but Tritzin wants Dad dead. The wind gusts, flinging sand into my eyes and dragging the clouds across the moon again. I turn back to Dad.

"Maybe we should turn back," I say.

"We have no more money. We need to get across."

"There might be other ways."

He is silent for a moment. "They know about the evidence," he says. "If we wait any longer they might get there first."

"He's got a gun, Dad," I say. "He knows we're here. He's waiting for us to try so he can kill you."

"We could wait until the boat starts to move, then charge into the water and try and get on it. It won't stop. If we surprise him we might get away."

"How long do you think it would take to get from here to the boat?"

"I don't know. Maybe only half a minute." Dad rolls on to his side and stares at me. "Do you think you could see that far?" he asks.

In front of me a small beetle inches along the sand, slowly and inevitably, from one side of the dune to the other. I watch it in the moonlight as it moves freely, changing its place on the earth. Small tufts of grass bend in the breeze. Memories swim around my mind.

"I never have," I say. "I don't know."

He sighs and rolls on to his back, staring at the empty sky for a moment. "I wonder if there's anything worth dying for," he says quietly, then he turns back to me. "It's your choice," he says. "We do whatever you think is best.

"I trust you," he adds. "Look as far as you can and make whatever decision you think is right."

26

AFTER

So I tell her.

"I have a gift," I say. "I was born with it and then my grandmother helped me develop it. It allows me to see what is going to happen."

Then I watch as her eyes widen. "What are you talking about?" she whispers.

"I think of it as stealing pieces of time," I say. "There is a way of keeping everything still in my head so that I can see what is going to happen in the world." I shrug. "It sounds crazy but it's true. I was able to see what would happen if I tried to jump on to that wall at the house. I was able to see what would happen when you attacked that man outside the post office and I was able to see what would happen if I crept into the corridor and looked for your mum's room. And that's how I knew."

She shakes her head and I wonder if she is going to cry. "Why would you say something like that?" she whispers. "Why would you make up something so stupid?"

So I tell her I will prove it to her.

"Think of something," I say. "Something private that I couldn't possibly know. Something that only you or your mum might know, but don't tell me what it is. Something with detail."

She is reluctant but eventually she agrees. "OK," she says. "I'm thinking of what colour dress I wore when Mum took me to *The Sleeping Beauty* ballet when I was five."

"OK," I say. "Now wait ten seconds and then say it out loud."

She stares at me, counting in her head, distrust all over her face. When she gets to ten she says, "Peach with white trim."

"It was peach, wasn't it?" I say. "With white trim."

Hayley stares at me. For a moment she has forgotten about where we are or what's happening as she tries to work out how I've done it. Then she shakes her head.

"It's a trick," she says. "How did you know?"

"I looked ahead until you said it. Then I knew what it was."

"But I didn't say anything," she says.

I nod. "Because I changed things by interrupting. If I hadn't, you would have said it and that's how I knew." But she still doesn't believe me. "Try again with something more complicated," I say. "Maybe a number or a fact or both."

Her chin moves slightly as she nods. "OK," she says. "I've thought of something."

I watch her and I can almost see the thoughts racing round her head. She doesn't believe me, and she can't understand why I'm saying what I am. She waits longer this time, but she could wait a year and it would make no difference. Eventually she says, "Eight minutes and forty-two seconds."

I repeat it back to her and now the distrust turns to shock. She stares at me.

"When I was born the doctor thought I had a problem," she says. "So they took me away from Mum to check me out. She said she counted every second and it was the worst eight minutes and forty-one seconds of her life. Dad wasn't there and she said she never told anyone because she thought it sounded silly. But then there was an accident at gymnastics training and I hurt my leg and she came to the hospital and told me. Nobody else knows it. Except you."

"I said forty-two seconds," I say. "You said forty-one."

She nods slowly. "I decided to say the wrong number, even though nobody knows the right one, and you still got it."

"So you believe me?"

She puffs out her cheeks and looks at me before nodding again. "How do you do it?" she says.

"I don't really know. It's to do with dominoes falling and the world turning and a whole bunch of stuff that I never quite got," I say. "I just know it works."

"How far ahead can you look?"

I look away for a moment. "It used to be a few seconds, but I worked out how to make it longer. Now I can go as long as I want."

"What's it like?"

I pause for a moment, wondering how to describe it. "It's like after you have been to see a movie," I say. "It is in your head and you know the detail of what happens. I don't need to rerun the whole film to recall a certain part, I just know it." I shrug. "And I can't change the future," I add. "I can only change what I do now to try and influence things. I have no control over other people."

"Does my mum know?"

I shake my head. "My grandmother and my dad are the only people I have ever really trusted," I say. "But I would like to trust you."

She looks a little scared then nods once. "You can

trust me," she says, and she smiles a short, sad smile. We sit in silence for a moment feeling the swell of the boat beneath us. Then she asks another question.

"Are we going to be OK?"

I am saved from answering as the throb of the engine suddenly dies. We both tense, forcing ourselves to listen to the movements on deck. Sometime in the last hour the sun has set and the only light that spills into the cabin is a weak glow from the moon above us. I feel the boat lose momentum then seem to rest on the water, rising and falling on the waves. Then the cabin door opens roughly and the mechanic is there, holding a gun, with Stripes behind him, shining a torch down into the cabin. The mechanic frowns when he sees our mouths free from the tape, but doesn't say anything, just moves quickly to open the door at the side and drag Rachel out. She doesn't fight, but comes out meekly, as if she is beaten. When she sees Hayley she nods slightly but there is no more signal than that.

The mechanic pushes her up the stairs on to the deck then returns to cut the tape round our feet so we can get up too. My legs ache from inaction, but

I force them to work, moving quickly to get to the stairs then out into the howling wind. We are in the middle of the sea with nothing around us. A strong wind hurries the clouds across the moon, and there are no other sounds except for the slapping of the waves against the boat and the idling of the engine.

There are two more men on the deck, a lookout at the tip of the boat and one in a small sheltered steering position. As I step on to the worn deck, he turns to look at me. And I can see it is Ronnie.

He turns and shouts down to Stripes. "You never said anything about the kids," he says, but Stripes doesn't care.

"It's been decided," he says. "There's no other way."

I catch Ronnie's eye and he stares at me helplessly. "You don't have to do this," I shout. "I got your passport. I went back for it."

For a moment he hesitates, but Stripes waves the gun at him. "Don't do anything stupid, Ronnie," he says. "This is happening. There's no way out now."

"They're just kids," Ronnie says, but Stripes shrugs.

"There's always kids," he says.

He tells Rachel to go to the side of the boat. She moves past me and I know what she is going to do.

I know that she has managed to free her hands and she is just holding them in place, waiting for the right moment, but I also know it isn't going to come. I scream at her to wait, but Stripes thinks I'm screaming at him and Rachel ignores me.

There are five of us now on the deck, with Stripes and the mechanic pointing guns at me, Hayley and Rachel, while Ronnie and the last guy stand further forward, watching silently. Stripes tells us to move to the side of the boat. Then he levels the gun.

"Wait," I scream again, but Rachel still ignores me. She dives forward at him, her hands free and reaching for the gun, stretching out desperately to stop him. It is all she has left but I know she is too far away and the only thing I can do is shove myself to the side, so that my shoulder pushes into hers just as she dives forward. It knocks her off balance as the gun goes off, shattering the night. Hayley screams as Rachel crashes into Stripes's legs. The boat lurches and they both tumble over. The mechanic raises his gun, but the movement of the boat delays him. He reaches out to grab hold of the rail and I rush forward, throwing myself at him as hard as I can, knocking him off his feet so that he lands hard on the deck. The gun falls from his hands and skids across the wet boards but I can't get to it quickly because my hands are tied.

I crawl across the rough white deck towards it as fast as I can, sliding on my bound wrists with the mechanic right behind me, but just as we both reach it there is a heavy thump as Ronnie jumps down on to the deck and picks it up. He orders us to stand still and stares at us, seemingly lost in indecision. Then another shot rings out.

We all spin round at the sound of the shot. Rachel is wrestling with Stripes but I can see she is hurt. Hayley has joined the fight but Stripes is too strong for them. He scrambles clear of both of them and raises the gun to shoot. But with one last, desperate effort, Hayley dives forward and slaps hard at his legs. He stumbles and sways with the movement of the boat. His arm comes up to fire, but then he loses his balance. As the sound of a shot explodes into the night for a third time, Stripes trips and falls backwards, crashing his head into the rail round the deck. He looks dazed for a moment and tries to focus, but I can tell he is stunned. Hayley runs up to him and rips the gun from his hand, and he can only half swing at her to stop her. He staggers just as the boat lurches again.

And he goes over the side.

The mechanic screams at Ronnie to shoot us, but Ronnie seems to make up his mind. He tells the mechanic to shut up and get in the cabin. I run to Rachel, who is struggling to get up. Her hands are covered in blood and her face is white with pain.

"It's my leg," she gasps. "I'll be OK but I can't move much."

Hayley rushes to her and drags her away from the side of the boat. The guy at the front is shining a torch into the water and yelling something in a language I don't understand and when I look over the side I can see Stripes floating in the sea. He is moving, but not much, just about managing to keep his head up as the waves crash over him. And he is floating away from the boat quickly. If he stays in the water much longer he is going to drown.

I tell the guy with the torch to jump in after him, but he looks at me as if I am mad. I yell at Ronnie to do something but he is busy watching the mechanic and shakes his head.

"Leave him," he says. "He would have left you." But I can't just watch him drown.

I hold out my hands for the guy to cut the tape

on my wrists, screaming at him to hurry until at last his eyes flick to Ronnie, who nods quickly. The guy produces a knife and cuts the tape and finally my hands are free. There is a rope coiled under the driver's chair and I grab it, telling him to tie one end to something. Then I grab the other end and dive over the side.

The water is colder than I expect and the waves are more fierce, crashing hard around me. Salt stings my eyes so I can hardly see. I scream at the guy on the boat to shine the torch, and the thin beam of light bounces on the surface of the water, rising and falling with the waves. I make sure the rope is wrapped round my wrist and force myself forward in the darkness, stretching out to find Stripes, but it is almost impossible. It is only when I reach the end of the rope that I finally see the white of his shirt, floating motionless in the water.

I shout to him as loud as I can but he doesn't respond and I can't even tell if he is alive, except I know that he is and I know I have to get him back. It is the only thing I am certain I need to do so I let go of the rope and force myself through the water towards him.

It is only a few metres but waves knock me off

course within seconds. With every moment away from the rope I can feel the panic rising within me. I know what is going to happen, but the terror still floods through me. I almost give up, but I don't. *Trust yourself,* Grandmother said, and so I force myself to be strong. I reach out and my hand strikes something. I grab it and pull it towards me, feeling the give in the fabric of Stripes's shirt, hauling it in towards me until I have it, then I slowly turn and head back to the boat.

They are coming back to us, but it still takes an exhausting minute to find the rope. Then I just cling on and let them drag me in. Eventually strong arms lean over the side and pull me aboard. While I lie on the deck panting heavily, someone checks Stripes' breathing. Then Hayley shouts that he's alive.

I close my eyes for a moment. And wonder what I have done.

After a minute I rouse myself and take stock. Rachel and Ronnie seem to have reached an uneasy agreement. She has strapped her leg up somehow and there is blood all over her jeans but she seems OK. Ronnie has thrown Stripes's gun overboard and he is now in control. The mechanic has given up the fight and the guy that threw the rope to me looks simply like he doesn't want to be there.

I turn to Rachel. "How are you doing?" I ask.

She shrugs, but I can tell from the way she sucks in her breath that she is in pain.

"She's OK but she's losing blood," says Hayley. "We need to get her to a doctor."

"Do we go back?" I ask.

Ronnie shakes his head. "We are about an hour away from France. It would be quicker to keep going," he says.

"Where to?"

"We have to keep going on the planned route. It was designed to avoid the shipping lanes. Otherwise there is too much danger of us being hit."

"Can't we just call for help?" Hayley asks, but Ronnie says no.

"Mobiles won't work until we are at the coast," he says. "We need to keep going and call when we see land."

There doesn't seem to be a better plan so we agree and get going. Ronnie watches carefully while the mechanic and Stripes are tied up. We treat them like they treated us, because it worked, except we take extra care over wrapping the tape round their heads so it can't be peeled off and I make sure Stripes is put on his side with no tape on his mouth in case he is concussed. He seems pretty out of it so we lock them in the cabin and go back to the deck. I get rid of my shirt and Ronnie gives me his dry sweater. I turn to say thanks, but he shrugs me away.

"Did you really go back for my passport?" he asks.

I take his and Ada's out of my pocket. "They're a bit wet," I say. "Sorry."

But he just laughs. "I didn't think I would ever get it back," he says. Then he looks across at Rachel. "And you think she will help us?"

I nod. "She's strong," I say. "And honest. And I trust her."

He grimaces a little then passes her the gun, then heads back to the driving area. Within a few moments the engine is throbbing again and we are on our way.

After everything, we are going back to France.

27

THE BEACH

We run. Keeping low, to the next dune, then we duck down again. I turn to Dad.

"Ready," I whisper.

He nods, but grabs my arm just as I am about to sprint off. "If anything happens to me," he says, "stick with Ronnie. He said he will get you to England."

"Nothing's going to happen to you, Dad," I say, wishing I believed it.

And now we've started, we need to keep going to the end. We need to see if it plays out.

He nods and I feel him tense. Then we are up and out, sprinting along the sand. Tritzin sees us almost immediately and his shout rattles through the air like a shot. I weave, trying to get as close to the boat as I can before darting into the water but every step also gets me closer to him. He raises his gun and an explosion rips through the night, but no one is hit. Noise bursts from the boat. Ronnie yells at someone to hurry and I watch as one of the smugglers reaches down to untie the boat from a buoy. The throb of the engine adds to the noise and the boat slowly starts to move. And we are still twenty metres away.

Tritzin shoots again, but again he misses. Dad jumps at the water, running fast through the waves until he is up to his knees. I am right behind him, taking long strides, trying desperately not to let the drag of the water slow me down. Tritzin is in the sea now too, trying to cut us off. He raises his gun again and this time a wave seems to knock him off balance. The shot splits the air but misses. And Dad is upon him.

Dad pushes him hard then keeps going, leaving him behind. Dad dives and I dive too, into the cold, my body flat in the sea so he can't see me. I push as hard as I can, kicking with soaked jeans, forcing myself faster against the waves and gradually the boat gets closer. I look up as I make my stroke, to see Ronnie standing at the back of the boat watching. It seems like he could pull away but he doesn't. My head plunges back into the water and I power my arms as hard as I can. The boat is closer. Another stroke, then another and then another. My hand hits the side of the boat hard and I pull my head out of the water, desperately trying to find a way up to the deck. Hands reach down for me. Arms from every part of the world. People who are scared and running reach down to help me, grabbing my hand and my clothes and anything they can to drag me on to the boat.

I look around, frantically trying to see Dad but there is no sign. I twist but someone screams at me to keep still. Then voices burst out and there is a flurry of movement on the other side of the boat. I can hear Dad and Tritzin struggling and cursing in my language and the smugglers shouting at each other to try to stop the boat from tipping. The boat heaves as people on the other side jerk away from the fight, then it suddenly rocks hard as a body scrambles on board. Dad's voice echoes through the night as he calls to me over the sound of the engine.

"Dad!" I yell.

"It's OK," he shouts. "I'm OK. We're going to—"

But another gunshot stops him.

He screams and falls hard on the packed deck. As people move to catch him, the boat tips in the water and people lurch to the side. Panic spreads quickly until Ronnie yells as loud as he can for everyone to sit down and keep still. I try to speak but one of the smugglers who can reach me screams at me to shut up and throws me down hard. I hit my head on the metal deck rail then collapse, just as a gun shatters the night once more and the boat finally starts moving. As I lie on the deck, dazed, I stare into the eyes

of an African woman who raises her fingers slowly to
her lips. Then somehow I can't keep my eyes open.
   And I pass out.

28

AFTER

The journey passes slowly. Despite the dry jumper most of me is soaking wet and the wind has really picked up so that it whips against my wet jeans, stinging like ice. The sea gets rougher too and we are forced to hold on to the rail almost constantly. After another half an hour the moon has disappeared behind thick cloud and we feel the first spots of rain. Soon it is torrential.

I stand with Ronnie most of the way as he follows a satellite navigation system, checking coordinates to a laptop and adjusting the boat's wheel frequently. We are sheltered by a screen from some of the wind and rain so after a while the others join us. Rachel looks at the laptop and asks how the navigation works.

Ronnie shrugs. "I only know how to go by the instructions," he says. "We have to follow the directions carefully to avoid hazards."

"What sort of hazards?" Hayley asks.

"Shipping lanes," he says. "And when we get near the land there are rocks." He adjusts the steering wheel slightly and I see the compass swing a little on the navigations system. "And patrols, of course," he adds.

Rachel is sitting at our feet, but she looks up sharply when he says this. "How do you know about patrols?" she asks.

"Whoever sets the course knows about them," says Ronnie. "I just follow the instructions."

But now Rachel is on her feet. "Where do the instructions come from?" she insists.

Ronnie reaches across and taps a couple of keys. "There's an email," he says. "There."

He points to the screen and Rachel almost gasps. "If there's an email, we can trace it," she says. She moves painfully until she can read what is on the screen. "There's only one person who has access to this information and knows I am a police officer," she says. "His name is Paul Booker and he's a Deputy Director at UK Border Force. This email is sent from an anonymous account, but if we can connect it to him at all, we've got him."

She leans back, breathing heavily, and I can't tell if it is with the exertion or with relief.

"And then it will be over?" Hayley asks.

Rachel nods. "Then it will be over," she says. She turns to Ronnie and me. "We will need you as witnesses and if you help us, we can help with immigration. So do exactly what I tell you, OK?" She smiles then lowers herself back down on the deck. "Let's get this boat to France and start putting things right."

Rachel and Ronnie stay in the cockpit and talk. At one point I go and check on Stripes and the mechanic, who haven't moved. Stripes stretches against his bonds when he sees me but he seems fine and I don't do anything. He has woken up a little and watches me carefully. "What are you going to do to us?" he says to me.

"Put that tape over your mouth if you keep asking questions," I say.

He goes quiet after that.

When I come back on deck, Hayley is waiting for me.

"Did you know what was going to happen?" she says quietly.

I nod.

"But you didn't change anything?"

I nod again and look down at the deck. "I couldn't think of anything better."

"It worked out fine though," she says with a smile. "You did really well."

I shrug. "Maybe."

Her smile melts away. "What?" she asks. "Have you

seen something else?"

I sigh and sit down on the deck, feeling the rain on my face and the boat rise and fall beneath me.

"Until today I could only see a few seconds," I say. "But now I can see more. I didn't realise what it would mean."

"What?" she says again. "What does it mean?"

"It means I know things I don't want to know," I say. "It means I see good things and bad things and things that could be either and I have to choose what to do. I can't look at every future, only a single path at a time, so how do I know my decisions are right? What if I choose something that seems right but leads to something much worse?"

She stares at me for a moment, then wipes her hair away from her face and sits down next to me.

"I don't know," she says. "You could stop looking."

I nod. "My grandmother said it's a gift and my dad said it's a curse. And I don't know which is right. Bad things are a part of life, aren't they? I can't stop everything bad happening but how do I know which things to try and change? What if I had a choice between losing you and your mum, or losing my dad?" I ask.

She turns and looks at me sharply. "Is that what you have to do?"

I look at her and lie. "No," I say. "But what if I did?"

She reaches across and takes hold of my hand, squeezing it between hers as she leans back and stares out at the water.

"I trust you," she says. "You won't get it wrong."

I look away, glad for the rain on my face to hide the tears.

"You know what I like to do most in the world?" she asks, and I shake my head. "Eat ice cream on the beach and watch the birds flying over the sea. How about when this is over we do that together and talk about this more?"

"I'd like that," I say.

And I smile, wondering why it hurts so much to do it.

Eventually we start to see lights along the French coast. Ronnie slows the boat and we all stare as hard as we can for a place to stop, but it is impossible in the darkness.

"This should be it," Ronnie says. "What do you want to do?"

"Just get us into the shore," Rachel says. "We'll get onto the beach and take it from there."

We push slowly through the water, listening as the roar of the waves gets louder until suddenly the boat crunches into the sand and shudders to a stop. I lurch forward, hanging on to the rail then stand up. The boat rocks in the swell but won't move any further.

"Time to get off," Ronnie says.

We untie the feet of Stripes and the mechanic, then jump down into the water. Rachel gasps as she lands but ignores the pain and we move in single file through the waves to the shore. As we get closer we can see streetlights up on the cliff to our right and hear the sound of traffic above the waves. I stagger forward, shivering with cold, holding the laptop high above my head, watching Rachel leaning on Hayley in front of me and just desperate for it all to end. Then I am no longer in the water, I am on sand. I stumble slightly as I push against waves that are no longer there until I can move freely at last. Ahead is a path that leads away from the beach and we move towards it.

"Not far now," Rachel says, and I can feel her spirits rise. Until the headlights of a large vehicle suddenly flood the beach with light. And five men get out, all pointing guns right at us.

"Nobody move," a voice shouts in English.

"I'm a police officer," Rachel shouts back. "*Je suis policier.*"

"Everybody get down on the ground," the voice shouts, and we all do it. We wait as the man approaches through the blinding headlights of the truck. Then Rachel gasps as his features become clear. He is clean shaven and handsome with short grey hair and bright blue eyes. It is the man from the house and from Rachel's reaction it is a man she knows. The man behind the whole operation. Paul Booker.

He is dressed in some kind of navy blue uniform under a thick black coat and he stares at us while we shiver in the cold and the men with him keep their guns pointed right at us. Rachel starts to shout something about murder, but he ignores it and one of his men comes up to her and shoves his gun in her face.

"Shut up," the man says, and it is clear he will shoot her if he needs to.

Booker walks up to Stripes then takes a knife from

one of the men and cuts the tape on his hands.

"You were supposed to report in," Booker says. "I figured something must have happened."

"Those stupid kids," Stripes says. "And we can't rely on Ronnie any more."

Ronnie stiffens but holds Booker's gaze as the tall officer comes up to him. Then he reels back as Booker smashes the handle of the gun across his face.

"Don't you realise how much you could have made? This won't be good for that family of yours."

Blood pours from Ronnie's face and he doesn't answer. Booker just shakes his head. Then he comes over to me.

"Who the hell are you?" he hisses, grabbing the laptop from my hand.

"Nobody," I say.

"Where's that accent from?" he says, and when I don't answer he shrugs. "It doesn't matter. Nobody will care about you."

"You won't get away with this," I say. "We've looked at your email. There's plenty of evidence connecting this to you."

For a moment there is panic in his eyes. Then he calms. "You might be right," he says. "It is an anonymous account, but maybe it's been compromised." He glares at Ronnie then takes a step away from us. "So I will delete it now," he adds. "And then there is nothing."

He turns to the man next to him. "Start getting them on," he says.

The man goes back to the truck and I hear the slide of a door opening, then, almost silently, people start moving down the beach. Person after person jumps down from the back of the truck then walks across the sand to the edge of the sea. The man strides out into the water, leading the way until they get to the boat, then he hauls himself up and pulls up the first of the migrants.

It is too dark to see them properly but I remember huddling in the boat, waiting to get to England. I stare at them and force the memories back into my head; how the fear claws at your mind, how each minute seems like a lifetime. And how you wonder how a new country can be worth this terror. But by then it is too late to turn back.

The boat sways and water crashes up over the sides, but no one says a word. The desperate cling to each other, more and more of them climbing up and squeezing on until every inch of the deck is covered but still the line snakes back into the water and they keep moving forward. Young men, strangers, families crushed together, all breathing the same salt air. I look up as they pass me and watch as they climb on and condense themselves like pieces of a puzzle. Faces hidden in a thick, howling, empty night. A wave rises high above the others and forces the boat up and then down, hard into the waves. It hits the water and everyone lurches forward. Hands grab for something to hold, but there are only soft, breakable bodies. The last few climb on and find the inch of space that they need. A moan rises up and fades into the roar of the sea.

But there are no words.

Booker has connected his laptop to his phone and opened the Internet. I can see the Gmail home screen glowing out of the darkness a couple of metres away. It seems to take some time to open the mail browser and then he is asked for a password.

I watch over his shoulder as he keys it in, before pushing Return to open a welcome screen. Then he spends about a minute deleting all the files and closing the account.

When it is done his eyes flick up to mine.

"There," he says. "All done. Now there is no connection and no evidence."

Then the man comes back from the boat. "That's all of them," he says. "Who's going with them?"

Booker grunts. "You'd better go. And take Charlie."

"I don't think I—" starts the mechanic, but Booker stares at him and he goes quiet.

One of the others comes up to them carrying the same black bag that Stripes gave to Ronnie and I just know it's got the passports and valuables in it.

"You want this?" he says.

Booker shakes his head. "No," he says. "Not today. Not any more. You and Razza take it back."

"But you always take it through in your car," the man complains. "Because they won't stop you. What if we get caught?"

Booker looks at Rachel, who is staring at him. "Not any more," he says. "This operation only happens because of me. I'm not going to take any more risks."

"I want more money then," the mechanic says, and Booker nods.

"Fine," he says. "Let's just get it done."

"And them?" Stripes asks, pointing at us.

"Do it in the water," Booker says. "There'll be less evidence." He passes him the laptop. "Throw this overboard when you get close."

He looks around one last time and nods briefly. Then he turns and heads back to the truck.

One of the men grabs Hayley by the shoulder and drags her to the water. Another one grabs Rachel, while the last keeps his gun trained on Ronnie and me. Rachel fights hard but she is injured and the man shows no mercy. He holds her at arm's length and drags her across the sand until they are up to their knees.

"It's OK, Mum," Hayley shouts. "It's going to be OK." But it isn't.

Rachel wrenches herself some space and reaches out, managing to clutch Hayley's hand for a moment until they are separated again.

I close my eyes because I can't bear to watch. I close them tighter than I have closed them before. It is the end of the journey and it is time to stop.

I close my eyes like I never want to open them again.

29

THE BOAT

Sometimes it's difficult to remember I am still the boy in the boat, drifting in the darkness towards England.

The boat heaves and water crashes up over the sides, but no one says a word. We cling to each other. The arms of strangers are wrapped round me and bodies lie crushed together, breathing the same salt air. I look up at the eyes of the families huddled across from me. Faces hidden in a moonless, starless, empty night. Large frantic eyes in bodies paralysed by the unknown. They are not from where I am from, but we are all black shadows, desperate and scared. The motor rips across the sound of the sea and forces the boat hard into the waves. We hit the water and our bodies lurch forward. Hands grab for something to hold, but there are only soft, breakable bodies. A moan rises up from around me.

But there are no words.

I am built from my memories. Of everything that has gone. My mother, my friends, my grandmother, my home, my life. They roll around in my mind until I don't know what is real and what is not. And what are memories that they can make blood and muscle and bones? What are memories that make me who I am? If I steal time, do I become someone else because new memories lie with the old, like broken bodies on a boat, tossed in a sea? If I know something in a memory, I know it forever because it is me. And memories that never happen are part of me too.

The boat banks steeply. Fingers grip at nothing on the deck. A child cries and a mother whispers but she can't move. We force ourselves through the sea towards a better future.

30

NOW

I open my eyes. The beetle makes it to the other side of the dune then disappears into a hole, and suddenly my mind is full of memories; of things that have not yet happened, stretching out into a future that will happen unless I make the right decision now.

"We can't get on the boat," I say.

Dad looks shocked. "But we must," he says. "They are looking for us. We need to get to England. We're not safe until we do."

"You said it was my choice," I say. "You said you trusted me. I am sure we shouldn't get on the boat, Dad. We need to go back to the camp."

I grab his arm before he can argue more. "You said you were going to trust me," I said.

"Yes but..." he starts, before stopping. "I did, didn't I?" he says. "And I do." He nods. "OK. Let's go back to the camp."

"And I need to use the phone."

He passes it to me and I check it. There is not much credit left and we have no more money but I dial the number anyway. Dad frowns when he sees it's international but he doesn't say anything. It rings several times and then a voice answers.

"Who is this?"

"You don't know me," I say. "But it's really important that you listen to me. Because you're in danger."

"Only two people have this number. How did you get it?"

"I'm afraid I really don't have time to go into detail. I'm on a mobile with about one minute before my credit runs out. But I know things that can help your investigation."

There is a pause. "I'm listening."

"Rachel," I say, "I'm on your side. You were right that there's a man on the inside. His name is Paul Booker and he's organising cross-Channel—"

"Paul Booker!"

"Paul Booker," I repeat. "He's passing border patrol routes to the smugglers so they can bring people across. There's a boat going tonight. I was supposed to be on it."

"Who are you? How can I trust you?"

I ignore the question. "If you want evidence, he sends emails from an anonymous Gmail account: ps113@gmail.com. The password is PA$$poRt17. That should give you enough to investigate further. And there will be physical evidence in his car when he returns from France tonight. He strips the refugees of valuables before they set sail, then brings them back himself because he can pass through the border without being searched."

She hesitates. "There was suspicion about Paul," she says thoughtfully, "but it went away." She thinks for a moment. "If I get this wrong it could wreck my career," she adds. "How do I know I can trust you?"

"Because I know you're a good person," I say. "Because I know you care about the people you are trying to protect. Because I know your daughter loves you and wants to be just like you. And I know the worst time of your life was the eight minutes and forty-one seconds when she was taken away from you. I know that anyone who loves their child enough to count those seconds will do the right thing and take a risk. If you don't act on this information my dad and I will be in serious danger, but I know you will. I will be at the Red Cross station in Calais tomorrow afternoon at two o'clock and my name is Aleksander S—"

But that's all I get before the phone runs out of credit. I stare at the phone, wishing I had said more, not knowing if it was enough. I should have said about the peach dress. I should have said about vinegar on her chips. I should have said more.

Because I can't make people do things. I can only wait and see.

31

LATER

She turned up about fifteen minutes early, flanked by two other officers, clearly nervous but determined. I'd been so scared all morning that she wouldn't show up that I just wanted to run up to her, but I held myself back because I still didn't know how she would react.

"Rachel?" I said.

She stared at me, wondering how I knew her, searching my face for any recognition but of course there couldn't be.

"How do you know who I am?" she asked.

"One of the people-smugglers knew your name," I replied, which wasn't exactly a lie, yet. "Can we talk about it later?" I said. "I really need to get my dad because he's in danger."

She nodded slowly and I led the three of them away from the football pitch into the town where Dad was sitting at the back of a coffee shop. We went in and crowded round a small table.

"Did you find the evidence about Paul Booker?" I asked.

Rachel nodded. "Emails going back years," she said. "And when we saw those, we stopped his car last night. A boatload of migrants were picked up on the beach and they've managed to match items of jewellery in his car to the people picked up. He's in a lot of trouble."

I looked across at Dad and smiled, but he still looked anxious.

"We need to get to England," he said. "There are people from my country looking for me because I have evidence of war crimes."

Rachel turned to one of the men with her and gave him a brief order to contact their office. "We have permission to take you back with us if you are willing to give evidence against the people-smugglers," she said. "We can get on the next train and debrief you in the UK."

And suddenly I could feel the relief flood through me.

Dad grinned and his shoulders seemed to shrink down as he breathed out hard. "Thank you," he whispered.

I smiled at her. "There's a man called Romek Andris who will help too," I said.

"Ronnie!" Rachel frowned, but I leaned forward to urge her to listen.

"He's a good guy," I said. "He's been trapped by Booker but he wants to get out. He knows all the details of the operation and he can help you put them all away."

"I thought Ronnie was beyond us," she said thoughtfully. "Maybe people change."

"Maybe they do," I agreed. I tucked my hands under my arms to stop them shaking. "Can we go to England now, please?"

32

LATER

We were fast-tracked through the system but even that took a week. First we were interviewed by asylum administrators, then the police and border patrol enforcement. At one point we were asked to identify Grandmother's necklace and told we could have it back after the trial. Then someone from a department that doesn't really have a name came to take Dad to the post office in London to collect his package. They told us that on Monday morning they arrested two armed men who turned out to be members of a foreign security service and were loitering outside. Both claimed diplomatic immunity but were expelled from the country. Once the British got the information in the package they spent two days locked in a room with Dad, going through it, asking a million questions about where the information came from. Dad told me later that they never said if it was useful or not, but they seemed pretty surprised by some of it. I hope it made a difference and helped some of the people at home, but maybe we will never know.

And while they were in the middle of that, our clearance came through to stay while our applications were processed. The centre doors were opened to let us out and Dad and I took our first free steps into

England. We didn't go far. We just went and sat on a bench in the middle of a small shopping centre and watched while the people around us got on with their lives. We didn't speak much either. First we sat close, then Dad leaned across and put his arm round my shoulder, pulling me in tight to kiss me on the side of my head. I thought we would feel like celebrating, but all of a sudden, the road ahead seemed as long as the one behind and this time we didn't really know where we were heading.

"We work hard and keep going," Dad said, as if he could read my mind. "And every day we should remember those that we left behind."

Later on, Dad had to go back and talk to the men in suits again so I found my way to Gatwick train station. There was enough in our allowance for me to get the train to Brighton and when I got there I walked to Rachel's house, even though I knew she would be out. When Hayley opened the door she stared at me with a blank face.

"You don't know me," I started. "But your mum rescued my dad and me in France. I wanted to come round to say thanks."

She crossed her arms and frowned slightly as she stood on the doorstep. "She's not here," she said.

I forced a disappointed look on to my face. "That's a shame," I say. "I owe her everything. We had to run from our country and then we were trapped. The people-smugglers had her information and I called her. She took a huge risk in believing me."

A puzzled look crossed Hayley's face for a moment and then she smiled.

"That was you?" she asked. "Mum said you helped her bring down the whole gang." Then her expression clouded. "She said it must have been bad for you. She said terrible things were happening in your home."

"There are terrible things happening in lots of places," I said. "And you should be very proud of your mum."

Hayley smiled. "I am," she said. "Although I don't tell her in case it goes to her head."

I smiled too and there was a pause while neither of us could think of anything else to say. Hayley shrugged and started to close the door.

"Would you like to go for a walk?" I asked, before it was quite shut.

"A walk?"

"I thought maybe we could go to the beach and eat ice cream and watch the birds," I said.

She looked at me and I didn't know if she was going to say yes, but I hoped she would. I remember thinking that it wouldn't be much of a story if you knew the end before you got there, so I stood still and waited for her answer.

I let it play.

Afterword

Running out of Time turned into a book about several things. It's a science fiction thriller; an exploration of choice and fate; the journey of a father and son; and in some part, it is also a story about the lives of refugees.

The journeys taken by refugees are hard and dangerous, and I haven't attempted to convey every part of these here. I read a number of books and articles to try and understand what it might be like for Alex or someone like him, and I found *The New Odyssey: The Story of Europe's Refugee Crisis* by Patrick Kingsley and *Voices from the 'Jungle': Stories from the Calais Refugee* by Calais Writers particularly helpful.

Whatever the economics and politics of the situation, I hope that everyone who is scared or desperate enough to leave their home behind can find a place of safety at the end of their journey.

Acknowledgements

Thanks to Tom and the Nosy Crow team, to Eve, and in particular Ludo, who saw something when others didn't. To everyone who helped along the way, including Maurice and Imogen, who encouraged and advised. To the Monkey and the Stinkpants and especially Naomi, who puts up with it all.